Rejuvenating the

By the same author

AROUSING ANNA

Rejuvenating Julia

Nina Sheridan

LIBRIS

An *X Libris* Book

First published by X Libris in 1995

Copyright © Nina Sheridan 1995

The moral right of the author has been asserted.

A CIP catalogue for this book
is available from the British Library.

ISBN 0 7515 1569 8

Photoset in North Wales by
Derek Doyle & Associates, Mold, Clwyd
Printed and bound in Great Britain by
Clays Ltd, St Ives plc

X Libris
A Division of
Little, Brown and Company (UK)
Brettenham House
Lancaster Place
London WC2E 7EN

Rejuvenating Julia

Chapter One

THE RICH IVORY silk of the lingerie shimmered under the cold, fluorescent lighting of the department store. Julia stroked her fingers across the front of a pretty, lace-trimmed camisole, wondering how the silk would feel against her naked skin.

Next to the camisole there were briefs, no more than a handful of lace and silk: a mere whisper of fabric, barely there. A matching suspender belt completed the ensemble, cut deep across the stomach to flatter and define.

Closing her eyes against the outrageous price tags, Julia imagined slipping into the beautiful garments, adorning her freshly washed and talcumed skin in silk and lace. Easing the glasslike stockings slowly up each leg before rising to greet her husband.

Michael would be startled, shocked perhaps, but how could he resist her dressed in such sensuous underwear? How could the sight of her fail to move him, even after all this time? Was this

1

the sort of thing *she* had worn? Michael would be sure to forget her if only Julia could recapture his interest, excite his flagging libido.

A smile touching her lips at the thought, Julia's hand hovered over the expensive lingerie set, her mind racing to try to work out how she could afford it.

'Oh Mum, do hurry up! We'll never find you a dress for the party if you stand there day-dreaming.'

Julia snatched her hand back as her daughter's exasperated voice reached her from across the aisle. A warm tinge of colour crept into her cheeks, making her feel angry with herself for feeling guilty. After all, *she* was the mother, Melissa the daughter, much though the positions seemed to have been reversing of late.

'What are you looking at?' Melissa had come up beside her curiously. 'Ugh, Mum – don't you think they're a bit tacky?'

'No I don't! They're beautiful.'

Melissa snorted with all the confidence of an eighteen-year-old.

'Not on someone your age they're not!'

Julia had a shocking, overwhelming urge to slap her pretty face, but Melissa had already moved on to the dress department. No doubt rooting out something suitable for someone 'my age'! Julia fumed silently.

'*No*, Melissa,' she said firmly as her daughter held up a floral two-piece for her approval. 'I'm thirty-seven, not seventy-three. I know exactly what I want for the party.'

'Don't know why you bothered to bring me

along then,' Melissa mumbled sullenly.

Suppressing the urge to reply that she didn't know either, Julia decided to abandon the shopping trip and come back on her own the next day. Walking back to the car park she wondered what had happened to change her relationship with her daughter. She and Melissa had always been close enough before. So why, suddenly, did they rub each other up the wrong way all the time?

Melissa went through the swing doors to the car park before her and Julia held the door open for a mother with a pushchair. As she went through herself, she heard a wolf whistle from the scaffolding above her. Glancing up automatically, her gaze clashed with a pair of laughing brown eyes in a young, tanned face. A very pleasant face, even-featured and openly admiring. The young man winked playfully at her and Julia felt herself colour up before she hurried away.

'Did you hear that guy whistle at me?' Melissa hissed as Julia joined her by the car.

'No,' she said vaguely, making a great show of fumbling for her keys to mask her expression.

'Think he fancies me,' Melissa said with satisfaction, sliding into the passenger seat.

Oh, the unshakeable confidence of the young! Julia sighed. Unable to help herself, she glanced over to where the workmen were busy repainting the woodwork. The whistler was still watching her and he grinned cheekily as her eyes widened in surprise. He couldn't be more than about twenty! Virtually the same age as her son.

For some reason she couldn't explain, Julia was

more flattered than annoyed by the young man's flirtation. And as she slipped into the driver's seat, she was ashamed to realise that she felt quite smug that it wasn't her daughter who had received the admiring attention. For once it was her. What was more, it felt good.

'I never thought you and Mike would reach twenty years! Not after that business with Michael and. . .' Louise, Julia's friend and neighbour, trailed off, realising that she had gone too far.

'Yes, well that was over a year ago,' Julia responded crisply.

She could feel Louise watching her as she bustled about, putting the finishing touches to the evening's buffet.

'Are you happy, Julia? I mean, you always put a good face on things, but have you really worked it out between you?'

'Of course. In fact, Gail is going to be at the party tonight.'

Louise whistled softly between her teeth.

'That's very . . . civilised of you.'

'We're civilised people.'

Aware that her voice was brittle, Julia softened her response with a smile.

'Pass me those vol-au-vents, would you, Louise?'

'Okay, I can take a hint! I'd best get back anyway,' she admitted, passing over a large plateful of the savoury pastries. 'It seems to take longer and longer each year to make myself look presentable.'

4

Julia laughed good-naturedly. Louise was the youngest-looking forty-year-old she knew.

'See you later.'

Upstairs in the bathroom, Julia stripped off and treated herself to a long soak in the bath. Closing her eyes, she sank into the soft, delicately fragranced bubbles and thought about Louise's question. *Had* she worked things out with Michael?

He would probably say they had. His 'little fling' with Gail Jones, the school secretary of all people, was now past history. A minor aberration in an otherwise flawless marriage. Julia grimaced. It wasn't really the affair that bothered her, not any more. It was the . . . emptiness, the awful, creeping suspicion that, somewhere along the line, something between them had died.

'Oh for Pete's sake!' she said aloud, hauling herself out of the bath and rubbing herself dry. 'I love him. I do. It's not his fault that I'm beginning to feel old.'

There, it was said. The truth that had been nagging at the back of her mind for weeks, no months, growing slowly, slowly into a conviction that life was passing her by.

Back in the bedroom Julia scrutinised her naked form in the full-length mirror. Not bad for a thirty-seven-year-old mother of two, she told herself defiantly. Her breasts were still reasonably high and firm, her legs a good shape. Heavier than in her youth, it was true, but then everyone put on a little weight over the years, didn't they?

Her hands smoothed across her stomach, undulating softly over its roundness, convincing herself it was womanly rather than fat. She had a few stretch marks, a legacy of childbirth, but over the years these had faded to faint silvery lines, barely noticeable.

There was nothing repulsive about her, nothing off-putting as far as she could see. So why didn't Michael seem to fancy her any more? Turning away with a sigh, Julia fetched the new underwear from the back of the wardrobe. The rustle of tissue paper sounded vaguely decadent and she smiled. Fancy having to sneak back into the store to buy it just so that her daughter didn't know!

As she had anticipated, the silk felt delicious against her skin, cool against her still bath-warm body. First the briefs, a wisp of silk and lace. The thong back felt odd at first, dividing the generous cheeks of her bottom into two distinct globes. After a while, though, the constant, gentle pressure on her sensitive skin felt quite pleasant.

The suspender belt sat on the swell of her hips, the deep-cut front holding her stomach in. Attaching the suspenders to the sheer, pale stockings, Julia admired the effect for a moment before slipping the camisole over her head. She had been worried, in the shop, that the lack of support would be uncomfortable, but all her doubts were expelled when she saw the way the silk skimmed her naked breasts. Their dark crests just showed through, hardening with a hint of the licentiousness which was already beginning to build within her belly.

Michael would be home from work soon, and at eight their guests would start arriving at the local church hall she'd hired for the evening to help them celebrate their twentieth wedding anniversary. Would this new underwear ensure that they would have their own, private celebration later?

Reluctantly, Julia covered it up with the simple, deep purple shift she had bought at the same time. Sitting at her dressing table, she curled her long, dark brown hair and applied make-up. Spraying herself liberally with Estée Lauder's *Private Collection*, she slipped into her shoes and went to make a cup of tea.

'You look nice, love.'

Julia looked up and smiled as Michael walked into the kitchen.

'I thought I'd better get myself ready before Melissa gets home and hogs the bathroom.'

'Hmm. Well, you know these young people – they like to look good.'

'So do some of us older ones,' Julia snapped tartly.

Michael paused in his excavation of the fruit bowl and raised a mildly questioning eyebrow at her.

'Right,' he said mildly. 'I suppose I'd better go and freshen up myself – you wait till you see what I've got you for our anniversary!'

He grinned and disappeared through the door. Julia could hear him whistling to himself as he bounded up the stairs. So he'd bought her a present. She smiled. That was a promising sign. Something romantic, perhaps, like a new nightdress, or perfume . . . or maybe jewellery? She discounted the last – a teacher's salary didn't run to jewellery, not after the mortgage was paid. Still, at least he'd bothered to get her something. She went about making the last-minute preparations with a lighter heart.

In the end, there was such a rush to transport everything over to the hall in time for the first guests to arrive that Julia barely had time to notice Michael until the party was well underway. Watching him laughing with her mother across the hall, Julia hugged to herself the secret of her planned surprise for him.

'You'd think Dad would have found himself something a bit sexier than that kit, wouldn't you?'

Julia looked up in surprise as her son, Gavin, swooped down and kissed her on the cheek.

'Oh, I don't know,' she laughed, hugging him hard. 'I think he looks quite good in that outfit.'

Leaving his arm affectionately round her shoulders, Gavin eyed his father's navy blue slacks and lighter blue silk shirt critically.

'He did – when you bought it for him . . . how many years ago?'

'Must be four.' Julia laughed. 'Oh Gavin, it is good to see you!'

Smiling, Gavin kissed her on the cheek.

'You too, Mum. How do you like the disco? Middle-of-the-road enough for you?'

'It's just right – an inspired present!'

'Good. I'll tell Nick – he had to search for hours to find all these "oldies"!' He laughed as she punched him playfully on the arm. 'You'll have to come and meet Nick later. He's on the catering course at college – I thought you might like to ask him about it.'

'Gavin, we've been through this before – I'm way past the stage when I could go to college,' she protested, aware that her son was not going to give up on her for a while yet.

'Rubbish,' he responded predictably. 'You're still a spring chicken compared to some of the mature students. Besides, you said yourself the job in the coffee shop is too limiting. What are you going to do with yourself when Mel leaves for uni? Speaking of my sister, who on earth *is* that with Mel?'

Glad to change the subject, Julia glanced across to where Melissa was making an art form of looking bored with a young man clad from head to toe in black leather. Everything about him was black, from his dyed, unbrushed hair to the kohl applied with a heavy hand around his eyes. As always when she saw him, Julia had to suppress the urge to laugh.

'Oh, that's Spider. Don't say anything, Gavin! Promise?'

He shook his head and moved aside slightly, making way for a group of women who had just arrived.

'Sally! Ann – Carolyn – you made it!'

Distributing hugs all round, Julia introduced everyone to Gavin.

'These are the girls who work with me at the coffee shop.'

'Mmm. No wonder you've kept him under wraps – I'd do the same if I'd got such a gorgeous son!' Ann teased and Julia was amused to see Gavin's ears turn pink.

'You should be ashamed of yourself, Ann!

Ann's getting married next Saturday,' she explained.

'Yes – and we've been trying to persuade your mum to come to my hen-night on Thursday. We're going to Goodfellas – it'll be a great laugh!'

'I'm too old for nightclubbing!' Julia protested self-deprecatingly, remembering Michael's amusement at the idea of her going.

'Rot! You tell her, Gavin – she's younger than some of the women who go to "grab-a-granny" night!'

'Oh thanks!'

'Go on, Mum – you don't get out and have fun often enough.'

Julia glanced up in surprise at Gavin's quiet encouragement. Had her son picked up on how dull and boring she'd been feeling lately?'

'Well . . . maybe,' she hedged, laughing as the girls all took that as a definite 'yes'.

Relaxing for the first time, Julia danced and chatted and laughed with all their friends and family. She even persuaded Michael to dance with her.

Laying her head on his shoulder, she closed her eyes and remembered how it used to be between them. Michael was the only boy she had ever wanted; together they had learned with love and tenderness all the delights their young bodies could bestow. God, how she had loved him!

Recalling all their hopes and dreams made her heart ache. They were going to buy a cottage on the coast where she would open up a tea shop and Michael would have a workshop. He would be a cabinet maker of the old-fashioned variety,

10

everything handmade and lovingly finished. Real life had never intruded in their dreams.

At seventeen and eighteen they were insatiable. Dancing was never enough, they had always been impatient to leave whatever village hall they had invariably ended up at, to tear at each other's clothes and roll in glorious abandon on the moon-dappled grass outside. . .

'Julia!'

Michael's mildly censorious tone made her jump and she realised she had been pressing closely to him, unconsciously rubbing her pubis suggestively against his.

'Sorry,' she murmured, moving away slightly before feeling angry at herself for apologising. *Apologising*, for goodness' sake! Remembering, though, had aroused her and she was suddenly conscious of the cool, slippery silk nestling into the moist, warm folds of her body, holding it in readiness for the night ahead, and she smiled to herself. She'd make Michael remember too . . . later.

When the song ended, Michael clapped his hands and called for everyone's attention.

'I'd just like to thank you all for coming tonight to help my wife and I celebrate our wedding anniversary. I'm sure you'll agree that Julia's done us proud with the buffet. . .' he paused as everyone applauded and Julia cringed, '. . .and now I'd like to present her with something I know she's been wanting for ages.'

There was an expectant silence as Michael led Julia by the hand to the trestle-table set up against one wall and the present laid upon it. Julia knew at once that it wasn't lingerie, or perfume, or any of the many things she had secretly hoped for. Trying to ignore the sinking feeling in the pit of her stomach, she unwrapped the brightly coloured paper in front of all their guests.

Conscious of Michael beaming expectantly at her, she forced a smile on to her frozen lips.

'Cast-iron cookware. Thank you, Michael. It's just what I've always wanted.' Though not as an anniversary present, she added silently, suffering his hug in front of everyone.

She was relieved when the disco started up again and Gavin came to her rescue, whirling her off for an energetic session on the dance floor.

'You all right, Mum?' he asked her afterwards as they went for a drink.

'Fine. Just promise me one thing, Gavin. Don't ever buy your girl saucepans as a present.'

'No chance!' he laughed, and as he left her to chat up a group of Melissa's friends, Julia was comforted to know that she would have no worries on that score. Gavin would make some lucky girl a great partner.

'You're looking thoughtful!'

Julia jumped as an unfamiliar masculine voice sounded close to her ear. Turning she recognised the friend of Gavin's who was running the disco. She smiled.

'Am I? That will never do, will it . . . Nick, isn't it?'

'That's right – Nick Lowther. At your service whenever you want to trip the light fantastic!'

He stuck out his hand and Julia shook it. His hand was warm, the skin unexpectedly soft. She remembered he was training to be a chef and guessed that he probably had to take care of his hands.

'Gavin tells me you're in the catering trade?'

Julia felt herself redden slightly at her son's exaggeration.

'Only in a very small way.'

'Oh.' Nick was regarding her thoughtfully, his head cocked slightly on one side. For some reason Julia noticed that he had the calmest, most tranquil-looking grey eyes she had ever seen, fringed by thick, dark blond lashes which matched his shoulder-length hair. 'We'll have to get together some time and swap recipes.'

Julia blinked in surprise. Was he flirting with her?

'Er . . . yes, maybe . . . I—'

'I see you two have introduced yourselves!' She was rescued by Gavin's timely arrival at her elbow.

Nick smiled, a slightly lopsided smile which Julia found strangely endearing.

'I'd better get back to the turntable,' he said, his eyes never leaving her face. 'Be seeing you.'

'Oh – yes.'

Julia watched as he made his way through the crowd towards the disco in the corner, forgetting, for a moment, that Gavin was beside her.

'Nice guy, Nick,' he said innocently and Julia snapped back to attention.

'Yes, he seems to be.'

Gavin smiled slyly.

'Good-looking too.'

'Gavin! I wouldn't know. For goodness' sake,

I'm a married woman, in case you'd forgotten,' she scolded, adding thoughtfully, 'Besides, he's young enough to be my son.'

'Not quite, Mum – Nick is one of those mature students I'm always telling you about. He's twenty-three.'

'Hardly ancient then!'

Gavin unexpectedly bent down to peck her on the cheek.

'Neither are you,' he countered, moving away before she had time to ask him what *that* was supposed to mean.

Looking around, her eye was caught by Michael dancing with Gail Jones of all people. Her lips tightened as she thought of how disapproving he had been when she had danced too close to him earlier in front of everybody. Apparently his censure did not extend to his former mistress – she appeared to be glued to him from the chest down. Unless she wasn't his *former* anything?

Julia pushed the horrible, suspicious thought away angrily. That was all behind them now. The fact that Michael could dance with the woman in public like that showed how far they had come. Noticing her mother waving hopefully at her from across the room, Julia pinned a smile on her face and dutifully headed in her direction.

Later, Julia lingered in the bathroom as Michael got into bed. Excited at the prospect of his reaction when she walked in dressed only in her new underwear and high heels, she dabbed fresh perfume behind her ears and prepared to make her entrance.

Michael had already climbed into bed. The soft glow of the bedside lamps cast romantic shadows across the duvet as Julia walked carefully across the carpet.

'Michael,' she whispered. 'Michael – would you like *your* present now?'

She frowned as no response came from the bed. 'Michael?'

Kicking off her shoes, she leaned over her husband's hunched shoulders, knowing before her eyes confirmed it what she would see. Michael's eyes were closed and he was snoring gently through parted lips.

'Damn! Damn, damn, damn you, Michael Penn!'

Scrutinising his features in the half-light, Julia's eyes scanned the thinning scalp, the recent, complacent pouchiness of his jawline, searching desperately for some resemblance to the beautiful boy who could never get enough of her body. Was he buried deep inside this . . . this man she barely recognised, just as the young girl she had been was still alive in her heart? If only she could catch a glimpse of it once in a while, maybe there would be some hope for them. But Michael seemed quite content to drift into complacent middle age.

Knowing from past experience that there would be no waking him, Julia undressed and enveloped herself in the comforting sexlessness of her cotton nightdress. Lying next to Michael in the gathering darkness, she stared up at the ceiling and tried not to cry. It wasn't just tonight – Michael falling asleep and the cookware – every other disappointment she had suffered over the past twenty years replayed itself through her mind.

How could she go on feeling so unattractive, so unloved? There must be more to life than working from nine until three in a coffee shop before coming home to cook dinner for the family which would be eaten, in silence, in front of the television.

An unwanted vision of tranquil grey eyes popped, unbidden, into her head and she pushed it away impatiently. There was no room in her life for mooning after the unattainable. Something Gavin had said was nagging away at the back of her mind. Her life had to change, it was inevitable. Now that Melissa was about to leave home, what on earth would she and Michael ever have to say to each other anyway?

Something else Gavin had said to her floated into the chaos of her thoughts. *You deserve a bit of fun.* Yes, she did. Only, she'd forgotten how to have fun.

Well, she was darn well going to relearn the art of enjoying herself. And the first step would be to go on Ann's hen-night on Thursday. The young man who had whistled at her in the car park the other day must have seen something in her. Just because her own husband never wanted her any more, it didn't mean she wasn't as attractive and desirable as she ever was. It didn't! All she needed was a little rejuvenation. Yes, that was it. Maybe a good dance and a laugh; a little mild flirtation was just what she needed to boost her flagging confidence.

She felt better for having decided something, but even so, it was a long, long time before Julia, lulled by Michael's deep, even breathing, fell into a fitful sleep.

Chapter Two

JULIA HESITATED AT the door of Goodfellas, feeling self-conscious in her safe black cocktail dress. Back home in the familiar territory of her bedroom she had convinced herself she looked pretty good. Her long brown hair skimmed her bare shoulders and the glimpse of cleavage the dress allowed looked, she thought, tastefully alluring.

Now, though, scanning the half-empty bar area, she saw that everyone looked so casual, and so very, very young, just as Michael had said they would.

'What do you want to go to a nightclub for?' he had scoffed when she'd told him she'd decided to come on Ann's hen-night after all. 'You'll stick out like a sore thumb. People will laugh and you'll make a total fool of yourself.'

At the time she had thought him petty and mean-spirited, but now she was here, she wasn't so certain. She couldn't see anyone of her own generation and no one seemed to have dressed up for the night as she had.

The music wasn't unfamiliar since Melissa played it night and day at home. But this loud, this incessant, it was little more than bearable. This nightclub bore little resemblance to the ones she remembered from the mid-seventies when no self-respecting nightspot was without a glitter ball, rotating slowly on the ceiling to reflect the disco lights on the dancers below. Suddenly she felt ridiculous. What *was* she doing here?

Anne, Sally and Carolyn were sitting on high stools by the semi-circular bar opposite the door. Just as Julia had decided she was going to slip away, unnoticed, Ann spotted her and waved from across the room.

With a smile fixed firmly on her lips, Julia went to join them.

'Hi – you look great!' Ann grinned, giving her a hug.

Julia eyed Ann's form-fitting Lycra tube dress and raised her eyebrows.

'I feel a bit overdressed,' she said in Ann's ear, the loud music making whispering out of the question.

Ann shook her head.

'You look gorgeous – really you do!'

'There can't be anyone here over the age of twenty-five!' she fretted.

'So what – relax, Julia, we're here to have fun!' Carolyn gave her arm a friendly tap. 'What are you drinking?'

'Um – what are you having?' Julia asked, looking at the bottle in Carolyn's hand.

Carolyn said something which sounded like

'Diamond Light' and Julia nodded. A light beer was probably exactly what she needed.

'I'll have a glass, though, if that's okay.'

The younger girls laughed good-naturedly and Julia joined them. How prissy she must seem! Some other women joined them then and Julia propped up the bar as she looked around her. The club was beginning to fill up now and more people were taking to the dance floor. Watching a group of young men dancing, Julia admired their raw energy.

She drank her first drink quickly and ordered another, just as Carolyn passed her another bottle. Gradually the room began to take on a faintly unreal glow and Julia realised that this light beer must be far stronger than she thought. She said as much to Carolyn and the younger woman laughed.

'That's not light beer, it's Diamond *White* – cider and white wine. It's about ninety-eight per cent proof!' She laughed at Julia's look of dismay before nudging her with her elbow. 'Look at Ann! Get in there, Annie!' She put two fingers between her lips and let out a shrill wolf whistle.

Following the direction of her gaze, Julia saw that Ann was dancing with a golden-haired six-footer who was clearly enjoying the attention. Julia's eyes widened as Ann wrapped her arms around his neck and began to gyrate suggestively with him, pelvis to pelvis. The girls on the hen-night went wild, forming a circle and slow hand-clapping as Ann moved her hands in mock passion up and down his body, rolling her eyes at them.

Julia watched from the bar, feeling self-conscious again. Glancing to her right from the tail of her eyes, she saw why. A short, balding man of around her own age in a loudly checked jacket raised his glass to her and smiled. Julia quickly looked away. Oh no, he was coming towards her! Automatically, she made a dash to the dance floor to escape him.

The other girls cheered and drew her into the circle they had formed. Ann was nowhere to be seen, neither was her golden-haired Adonis. Julia looked around worriedly as she jiggled awkwardly from foot to foot in time with the music.

'Stop being a mother hen and get this down you!' Carolyn said in her ear as she thrust another bottle into her hands.

Julia looked startled for a moment, then she grinned. Why not? It was only her vanity that made her think that anyone here was looking at her. Taking a swig from the bottle, she hiccuped and everyone laughed. Who cared? She was here to let her hair down. Apart from Carolyn, Sally and Ann, all of whom looked set to suffer severe memory loss in the morning, no one here knew her. There would be no one to face in the sober light of day. Finishing the beer, Julia allowed herself to feel the heavy beat of the music vibrating through her body and followed Carolyn's lead.

She liked dancing. It had been so long since she had really let herself go, and she had forgotten how good it felt. She was still a little tipsy, but it had been an hour now since her last drink and, having danced non-stop, she was fairly certain the alcohol was out of her system.

Sally leaned towards her and shouted that she was going to the bar again.

'Get me a fruit juice, would you? I'm so thirsty!' Julia yelled back.

Come to think of it, she could do with a visit to the Ladies' too. Weaving her way through the high-spirited crowd, Julia was conscious several times of attracting attention, generally male. Catching the eye of one dark-haired, casually suited man in the corner, she saw interest in his glance and felt her confidence increase. Michael was wrong – no one was laughing at her.

Catching sight of herself in the cruelly lit powder-room mirror, Julia grimaced. Her face looked hot and shiny, her hair was dishevelled. It didn't take long to put that right; a dusting of face powder, a rake of her handbag-brush through her hair and a fresh slick of lipstick and she looked as good as she had when she arrived. Better, now that there was a sparkle in her hazel eyes and a natural blush of colour to her cheeks.

A breath of air would be welcome, though, before she tackled the dance floor again. There was a bouncer on the rear exit door beside the Ladies' and he smiled at her as he let her through. Wandering a little way along the dimly lit alley, Julia was startled by a noise coming from one of the darkened alcoves. A soft, breathy cry which made her hesitate before glancing nervously back towards the club.

The bouncer was talking to someone inside and wasn't paying any attention to what might be going on in the alley. Julia knew she should quietly turn around and walk away, but the breathy little noises coming from the shadows intrigued her.

Tiptoeing closer, she put her hand to her mouth as she saw Ann. She was standing with her back to the brick wall. Her face was illuminated by a stray beam from a weak streetlight, her expression intense. Her eyes were closed, her lips parted. Blonde hair lay in disarray around her shoulders and Julia's shocked eyes were drawn to where her generous breasts rose and fell with her quickened breathing. The skirt of her short dress was bunched up around her waist and the golden head of the man with whom she had danced was buried between her thighs.

As Julia watched, Ann began to writhe, grinding her hips against his face and moaning softly. Julia fidgeted slightly as she imagined his rough tongue rasping along the inner creases of Ann's most sensitive flesh. Her own sex felt heavy and moist as she thought of how Ann must feel and it was hard to resist the urge to press her hand against herself through her clothes. Moving back slightly so that she was concealed by shadows, Julia stroked her palm firmly from her stomach to the gentle mound of her sex.

The other woman's face was transformed now into a picture of approaching ecstasy. She arched her neck, exposing her soft white throat, and her head began to move from side to side. Little keening noises came from between her parted lips.

Julia felt hot all over, impatient now with the

layers of crêpe and silk covering the swollen membranes between her legs. Her eyes widened as, tangling her hands into the man's hair, Ann held him close to her, gritting her teeth as if in pain as the first wave of her orgasm broke.

Imagining how she would feel if she found herself being watched during such an intimate moment, Julia pulled her eyes away with difficulty. Once it was over, Ann would open her eyes and see her; the alley was too narrow for Julia to pass them without their noticing. Reluctantly, she hurried back along the alley. The doorman grinned cheekily at her as she passed and Julia felt her cheeks flame. Did *he* know what was going on further along the alley?

Returning to the Ladies', Julia regarded her flushed cheeks and bright eyes in the mirror above the sink. She felt . . . shocked by what she had seen – after all, Ann was to be married in less than a week and Julia was surprised at her. And yet she wasn't nearly so shocked as she thought she would have been. Far, far stronger than that was the other reaction the scene she had witnessed had provoked. Arousal.

Staring at her reflection, Julia realised that her mouth felt dry, her breasts heavy and swollen. She could feel her nipples pressing against the flimsy fabric of her dress, see, quite clearly, their outline as she stood back from the mirror.

As she moved, her silk undies pulled against the delicate folds of her sex, the swollen lips rubbing slightly against the slippery fabric. Oh God, how was she going to go back out there? Anyone could look at her and see the state she was in!

24

Feverishly, she ran her wrists under the cold tap and splashed some water in her mouth. The doors swung open and a group of girls came in, giggling and jostling good-naturedly for elbow-space by the mirror, leaving Julia no choice but to leave.

'We were going to send out a search party!' Carolyn said as she emerged.

Julia took the glass of fruit juice Sally passed her and gulped at it gratefully.

'Has anyone seen Ann? She disappeared ages ago.'

Julia avoided their eyes and shook her head, sure that her cheeks were flaming.

Carolyn shrugged, unconcerned.

'It's her hen-night, for Christ's sake – maybe she's having a final fling! Hey, c'mon – I like this track! Who's for dancing?'

Julia followed the other two back on the dance floor, glad the subject had been changed. But she couldn't get rid of the image of Ann's face as she was brought to orgasm by the blond stranger. The unexpected sexual arousal she had experienced had by no means completely receded. It simmered below the surface, making her limbs fidgety with tension. Every movement made her conscious of the heaviness in the pit of her stomach, and of the silk panties which, once moistened, had moulded themselves to the contours of her sex.

It was a few moments before Julia noticed that there were now two men dancing with their small group. One, dark-haired, blue-eyed, the same height as her in her high heels, seemed to be

25

paying her particular attention. He smiled at her, displaying white, even teeth and an endearing dimple, and Julia automatically smiled back.

'Hi – I'm Paul. What's your name?'

He had to lean forward and virtually press his lips against her ear to be heard above the music. Julia caught a waft of fresh male sweat and apple-scented shampoo, a not unpleasant combination. His warm breath in her ear made her shiver.

Turning towards him, she mouthed 'Julia' and he grinned, moving closer to her. His hands came about her waist and they began to move in unison. It had been years since Julia had danced with anyone other than Michael and at first she felt a little awkward. But Paul clearly had no such inhibitions, for he drew her closer.

It was a heady experience, being held in another man's arms. Especially one so young, so vital as Paul. Studying him surreptitiously, Julia guessed he was probably twenty-two or three. Beneath his denim shirt, she could feel the tightly muscled shape of a man who worked out regularly and, without thinking, she ran the palms of her hands from his elbows to his shoulders and back again.

Paul's response was to begin caressing her back as they danced. His touch was featherlight, but sure, and Julia found she liked the experience. His denim shirt was damp from his dancing. She'd never thought that sweaty men were to her taste, but for some reason she found this particular man's body heat powerfully erotic. Perhaps it was the state she was in, heightening her senses,

26

making her more conscious than usual of the essential maleness of him.

The music moved up a tempo and Paul's hands moved more freely over her body.

'God, you're beautiful,' he muttered feverishly in her ear, his hands moulding and shaping her buttocks before moving up to her back again.

'So are you,' Julia murmured, her hands finding a path of their own.

His back was well-shaped and strong. Beneath the denim his skin felt smooth and hot. Stroking the back of his neck, Julia let her fingers rasp across the short, dark hair at his nape before moving up to shape the contours of his skull.

Julia could not believe how aroused she was, just through dancing with him. As she traced the shape of his ears with her fingertips, Paul cupped her cheek with one hand and brought her face round to his. His kiss took her by surprise, but it was more than welcome. As he pressed her to him, she felt the unmistakable tumescence at the front of his jeans and exalted in it. Somehow, knowing that she had turned him on was even more exciting than her own arousal.

Coming up for air, Julia caught a glimpse of Sally, Ann and Carolyn, still dancing, their expressions a mixture of surprise and amusement.

'Who are they?' Paul asked, following the direction of her glance.

'Workmates – it's Ann's hen-night. I don't usually come here. . .'

He looked over his shoulder and grinned at the other girls before easing Julia further away.

'Who wants to talk to them when I have a gorgeous thing like you to dance with?'

Julia laughed. She didn't know what else to do. The sane, sensible part of her mind told her that, the way she was behaving, Paul probably thought all his birthdays had come at once. But the wild, sensual woman she normally kept well buried didn't care. She knew she ought to feel shocked at herself, she ought to act like a normal, sensible, thirty-seven-year-old wife and mother. Only she didn't *feel* like any of those things. She felt . . . young again, certainly. Powerful, in a way she hadn't felt in a long time.

Here was a young man who had seen something in her that he liked. He knew nothing about her, only that, physically, he was drawn to her, just as she was to him. Crazy though it seemed, she didn't want to know anything more about him than that. What she felt was pure, unadulterated lust and, what was more, it was a good feeling.

His face was inches from hers. He filled her senses – the scent of him, the taste of his lips, the feel of his hard, firm young body pressing against hers, the potent thrust of his masculine arousal. Julia had the sudden, shocking urge to drop to her knees and unbutton his fly. She would release his penis from the confines of his jeans and caress it, rub it against her cheek. Then she would open her mouth and slip it inside. . .

He kissed her again, only this time he swept the inside of her mouth with his tongue, drawing the sweetness from her and clasping her at the back of her head so that she couldn't move away, even had she wanted to.

Julia could feel waves of weakness breaking over her arms and legs and she clung to him, mindless of the dozens of people dancing all around them. Was this how Ann had felt before going into the alley with the golden-haired stranger? She wanted him, God, how she wanted him! Her entire consciousness seemed to be concentrated on the heavy, rhythmic pulse which beat between her legs. With barely a thought for their surroundings, Julia folded her fingers around his and guided them between their tightly pressed bodies to the centre of her.

She felt the tension in him as he realised what she wanted and for one awful moment, she thought he was going to pull away. To her relief, he was merely glancing around for a suitable place where they could have at least some privacy. As he put his arm around her and drew her into the deep shadows in the far corner of the dance floor, she felt the excitement he was barely holding in check, and the knowledge that he was as affected as she spurred her on.

Though the music was fast and lively, Julia and Paul swayed gently, pressed close together, oblivious to the bodies gyrating all around them. His breath was hot in her ear, his breathing quick and shallow. Discreetly, he ran the tips of his fingers from her belly to the apex of her thighs, up and down with tantalising slowness. The referred stimulation of her labia and the hardening core of flesh hidden within made Julia's entire body suffuse with warmth.

It wasn't enough. She wanted to feel his fingers on her bare skin, slipping inside her heated folds of flesh. As if reading her mind, Paul began to pull up the front of her dress, manoeuvring her so that she had her back to a wall and his body shielded her from casual glances.

The first touch of his fingers on her exposed flesh was so electrifying that Julia almost came there and then. Her legs went so weak that she had to cling to him, leaning against his sturdy body to stop herself from falling over.

He kissed her ears, her neck and her face, murmuring gentle obscenities as she pressed against him, eager for more than the teasing play of his fingers across her belly. The elastic of her panties proved to be no barrier for his questing fingers as they ran slowly through the light mat of silky hair frosting her mound. She gasped as his first two fingers eased between the moist, swollen folds of her sex-lips and unerringly found their target.

It had been so long since Julia had last experienced orgasm and she was, by this time, at such a high pitch of arousal that she realised it would not be long before she came. A fine film of perspiration broke out all over her body as the crisis loomed. In a moment of pure, crystalline perception, she was aware of the insistent beat of the club music, the heaving, constant motion of those around them on the dance floor and the wholly personal vibrations of her own body as she raced towards the peak.

For all that she knew it was on its way, the strength of her climax took her by surprise. Sagging against Paul, she was unable to prevent a loud gasp from escaping through her lips. Paul crushed his mouth down on hers, swallowing the sound so that she could feel it reverberating in her throat.

Julia was only partly aware of him readjusting her clothing before he brought his hand to cup her face. She could smell the sweet, musky scent of her body on his fingers and she shivered.

This time when they broke apart, they gazed into each other's eyes for what seemed like a long time. Julia could feel the tension in him, see from the expression in his eyes that he was as surprised by the strength of his reaction to her as she was by hers. His eyes held a question, a hope.

Julia smiled, her hands roving his neat, denim-clad buttocks before coming round, briefly to caress his erection. His eyes widened momentarily, then they closed and Julia caught a brief, delicious glimpse of how his climax would transform his face. It sent a fresh rush of moisture to her sex and she knew that she had to have him, she simply *had* to!

'I'm going to the Ladies' – wait for me by the door?'

Paul nodded, his fingers clutching at hers as if he was reluctant to let her go. Julia wove a path through the crowds to the powder-room. Before she left the toilets, she fed some change into the condom machine on the wall and put a packet in her bag.

Catching a glimpse of herself in the mirror, she paused. Would anyone looking at her be able to guess what had just happened to her? She thought so; her eyes were heavy-lidded and overbright while two hectic spots of colour tattooed her cheeks. It had been a long, long time since she had seen her lips so red, or so full and swollen. Poking out the tip of her tongue, she moistened them, remembering the brief, yet shockingly potent fantasy in which she had indulged while on the dance floor.

Now was the time to back out, if she was going to. Now was the time to let common sense take over. She couldn't fool herself now that she had been carried away by the unaccustomed drink, or the atmosphere, or anything else if she went through with this. It was a cool, clear-headed decision.

She smiled. For once in her life she was going to follow her instincts and do exactly as she pleased! The very idea sent a thrill of anticipation through her so strong that it made her stomach tremble. Promising herself that there would be no more soul-searching, at least not tonight, Julia blew a kiss at her reflection and sauntered out of the door.

Chapter Three

SHE EXPERIENCED A moment of panic when she thought he wasn't waiting for her, then she saw him, pacing the entrance foyer, and she smiled to herself. Pausing, she took the chance to study him before he noticed she was there.

He wasn't a tall man by any means, no more than five feet eight or nine. But he was well-built, his shoulders broad and his chest pleasingly convex. He held himself in such a way that made him look as though he was taking up his fair share of space, giving the illusion of extra height.

Julia had always had a liking for very dark men. Her fingers tingled in anticipation as she contemplated Paul's thick, almost black hair and the tanned, olive-tinted tone of his skin. The shadow on his jaw suggested that he had to shave twice a day, despite his youth. Julia had a quick, delicious premonition of how that strong, square chin would feel rasping gently over her naked skin. . .

As if feeling her eyes on him, he turned then

and caught her gaze. His own dark blue eyes narrowed as he recognised the pure lust in Julia's appraisal. Then he smiled, a slow, enigmatic smile which did strange things to her equilibrium.

'Ready?' His voice was low, husky, caressing her senses. She nodded and stepped forward, putting her hand in his as he stretched it towards her.

They were lucky – it took mere minutes to find a taxi. A Ford Sierra, private hire, whose seats, though they looked clean enough, smelled of stale tobacco and beer. It didn't matter, for as soon as he had given the driver his address, Paul drew her to him. Julia lay her head in the convenient cup of his shoulder and closed her eyes for a few seconds. She liked the way he smelled; of light, spicy cologne and sweat and a heavier, muskier fragrance underlying the rest which she knew was due to his arousal.

Sighing happily, she allowed him to tilt back her head and plunder her mouth again, drawing in his hot, searching tongue and sucking at it gently. His hands were roaming her body, first smoothing down her back, then polishing her hip-bone with his palm. Tracing the line of her jaw, he brushed past her breasts to the soft undulation of her belly which she automatically pulled in.

Breaking the kiss, he smiled at her in the darkness.

'You are so, so beautiful,' he whispered, his warm breath fluttering over her ear and down her neck.

Though the words sent a ridiculous thrill through her, Julia laughed.

'I bet you say that to all the girls!' she teased, refusing to accept his casual flattery.

'No,' he said, quite solemnly. 'No I don't.'

She scanned his eyes, reading the sincerity of the moment in them and she warmed to him.

'Flattery will get you everywhere!' she murmured, leaning against him and initiating another kiss.

'This is it, isn't it?' The driver's voice, low, cultured, broke into their mutual absorption. Paul looked out of the window, visibly distracted, before nodding and reaching into his back pocket for the fare. Julia let him pay, watching his face as he said goodnight to the driver before opening the door.

Once they were both on the pavement, he took her by the elbow in a curiously courtly gesture as they crossed the road. The weather had altered so that there was a slight drizzle as they ran up the wide steps of the three-storeyed Edwardian terrace where he lived.

'Mine is the top flat – we'll have to be quiet as we go up the stairs!'

Somehow knowing she had to be quiet always gave Julia the urge to shout and she had to stifle a giggle as she ran quickly up two flights of stairs with him. She felt like a schoolgirl, sneaking up to her boyfriend's bedroom when his mother wasn't looking.

The communal areas of the house were painted a restrained green and there was a faint but all-pervasive scent of pine disinfectant hanging in the air. Once inside Paul's flat, Julia looked around her with interest.

From the state of the furniture Julia guessed that it was rented with the flat. It was shabby and old-fashioned, though Paul had made some effort to cheer the place up by draping the sagging sofa with a brightly coloured throw. There were books piled high in higgedly-piggledy towers to one side and a guitar was propped against an ancient-looking television set. Through an open door at the far side of the room, she could see a minute kitchenette, furnished in pea-green formica.

'Would you like a coffee?'

She smiled at him, sensing his sudden awkwardness.

'That would be lovely. I'll sit here, shall I?'

She sank down on to the lumpy sofa where she had a good view of him moving about the kitchen. While he waited for the kettle to boil he rinsed two mugs which had been standing on the draining-board. Feeling her eyes on him again, he turned and smiled at her before spooning in instant coffee.

He raised the sugar bowl and Julia shook her head.

'Just milk, thanks.'

The atmosphere in the room was tense as Paul carried the two mugs into the living-room and sat down next to her.

'Are you warm enough?' he asked her, glancing at the unlit gas fire.

'I'm fine. Can I ask you something, Paul?'

'Sure.'

'Do I make you nervous?'

He blinked, as if her question had taken him by surprise.

'Do I seem nervous?'

Julia smiled, putting down her coffee cup and reaching across to cup his cheek.

'A little,' she murmured, noting the sudden tension in his jaw. Smoothing her forefinger along it, she delighted in the rough texture of his skin where his beard grew.

'Should I be?' he asked her, his voice equally soft. Julia took his mug away from him and set it down on the coffee table next to hers. Looking deeply into his eyes, she slipped her hand into the opening of his shirt and rested it against the strong, steady beat of his heart.

'You'll just have to trust me, won't you?' she whispered.

Drawing his head down to hers with her other hand, she kissed him, savouring the taste of his firm lips and coaxing them apart with the tip of her tongue. Bringing her hand up from his chest, she placed two finger gently against his Adam's apple and felt the vibration in his throat as he let out a little groan of desire.

'Mmm – you taste good!' Julia whispered as they broke apart.

Opening her eyes, she saw that he was looking at her, his eyes, darkened now to navy, watchful as he waited for her to make the next move. Being in the driving seat, so to speak, was a new experience for Julia and, to her surprise, she found the position gave her a deep, atavistic thrill. Wondering whether the feeling she had of control was no more than an illusion, she decided to put it to the test.

'Let's go through to your bedroom,' she

suggested, conscious of the slight breathiness in her voice which betrayed her excitement.

Without a word, Paul stood up and held out his hand to her. It was an attractive hand, strong and tanned, the fingers long and square-tipped. His fingernails were cut short, spotlessly clean and a sparse smattering of dark hairs furred the space between each knuckle along the fingers. It was warm and pleasantly dry as it closed around her fingers.

The bedroom was small, dominated by a double bed and a huge, dark oak wardrobe which seemed to loom over everything in the room. Julia looked on approvingly as Paul went over to the bed and switched on the twin, red-shaded lamps at either side, bathing the room in a soft pink glow.

'I could do with a shower. . .' he said, trailing off as he saw the way she was looking at him.

He looked magnificent. The way he held himself; shoulders relaxed, yet his arms held slightly away from the sides of his body. Julia, relishing the potent, musky scent of his body drew it deeply into her lungs, intoxicated by it.

There was an energy, a vitality about him which acted as a powerful spur to her desire. Julia could not remember wanting anything as much as she wanted this virile, vital young body standing in front of her.

'Don't,' she whispered.

'Don't. . .?'

'Don't shower . . . don't move at all. I want you just as you are.'

She heard his sharp intake of breath and knew

that her words were having as strong an effect on him as her thoughts were on her. Advancing towards him slightly, she sensed his tension, knew he could barely control the swift flare of his arousal.

'Take your shirt off.'

His eyebrows shot up, his face registering shock at her forthright demand.

'Take my shirt off?' he repeated, as if not sure he had heard her correctly.

'I want to see you naked.'

He hesitated for a moment, then his fingers moved slowly to the pearlised buttons of his shirt. Julia's mouth felt dry as he began slowly to slip each button through its buttonhole and his bare chest was revealed.

As she had expected, it was covered in a light frosting of crisp, dark hair. It grew in whorls around the flat brown discs of his nipples and arrowed enticingly down to the dark indentation of his navel before disappearing into the waistband of his jeans. Peeling the still sweat-damp shirt off his shoulders, he turned the sleeves inside out as he pulled his hands through. Dropping it carelessly on the floor, he looked at her expectantly, waiting for her to tell him what she wanted him to do next.

'Turn around,' Julia whispered, her voice trembling slightly.

Her whole body felt tremulous as he slowly complied. How far dared she push him – how far would he go? Julia ran her eyes appreciatively over the broad sweep of the back now revealed to her. The skin was smooth and blemish-free, lightly tanned, the musculature well-defined. Julia's fingers itched to stroke the taut flesh across his shoulder blades, but she held back.

'Face me now.' She waited until he had turned slowly back again before moistening her dry lips with the tip of her tongue. Her eyes strayed to the thick, well-muscled thighs flaring from trim hips and she felt herself grow warm. 'Come here.'

Paul moved towards her without saying a word. The atmosphere seemed to crackle around them, the sexual tension binding them almost claustrophobic in its intensity. He stopped, inches away from her and regarded her expectantly.

For a moment Julia felt like a kid let loose in a sweet shop – she didn't know where to begin. Tentatively at first, supremely conscious of Paul's eyes monitoring every nuance of her expression, she reached out a hand and laid it gently against the dip in his chest between the pectorals.

His skin was hot, slightly damp so that her fingertips slipped easily across it. Glancing into his face, Julia reassured herself that he was willing to allow her to explore before bringing both hands together and running them quickly over his chest. Paul closed his eyes briefly, and when he opened them his expression was inscrutable. He watched her as she shaped and squeezed his firm flesh, tangled her fingers in the densest part of his chest hair and played with his nipples.

Julia was fascinated by their responsiveness. One minute they were flat brown discs, set symmetrically on the two neatly divided halves of his chest. The slightest pressure of her finger pads and they sprang to life, two hard little nubs of wanton flesh which pushed themselves outward, inviting further caresses.

It had been a long, long time since she had had a young, virile man to play with. Even before her sex-life with Michael had died, Julia had become used to a weekly routine which was hardly designed to set the world alight. She simply had neither the energy nor the inclination to explore and experiment with Michael. She wondered what his reaction would have been had she tried.

'Do you mind?' she whispered, stroking the tips of her fingers back and forth along the line of his collar bone.

He smiled, a slow, lazy smile which sent a thrill zinging right down to her toes.

'Do I mind?' he repeated softly. 'Are you kidding?'

His head dipped and his mouth found hers. But Julia wasn't interested in kissing him, not yet, and she moved away.

'I want you to stand very still,' she told him, slipping the thin straps of her dress over her shoulders as she talked. 'I want to explore every inch of you, bit by bit, and I don't want you to say a word. Will you indulge me, a little?'

His throat rippled as he swallowed.

'I'll try,' he promised.

Underneath her dress, Julia was wearing the cream silk underwear she had bought for her anniversary party. The light of appreciation in Paul's eyes as it came into view was gratifying, especially given Michael's indifference.

For now, though, having had her first flare of

41

passion assuaged, Julia wasn't interested in her own pleasure, she only wanted to touch and taste the man standing, ever watchful, yet deliciously compliant in front of her. Moving closer, she breathed in the heavy, animal scent of him as she splayed her hands across his chest again. This time she ran them up to his shoulders and down the length of his arms, all the time conscious of the shape of his muscles and the texture of his skin.

It fascinated her, the strength confined by such softness, the springiness of his flesh beneath the silk of his skin and the immoveable underlying muscle. Moving round him, Julia stroked his back, her long fingers sweeping inward to meet at his spine in the smell of his back, then moving upwards and outwards again, her fingernails raking lightly across his skin.

The gentle scratching brought him out in goosebumps. He liked that! Julia smiled to herself, storing the information away for future reference. Giving into the urge to press her lips against his skin, she felt the shiver which ran right through him.

She could taste the sharp, salty tang of sweat on her tongue as she made her way, bone by bone, from the middle of his back to the top of his spine with small, pressing kisses. Once at his hairline, she nuzzled the warm, sensitive spot where his hair grew in a tender vee at the nape before making her way back down his spine, between each vertebra this time.

As she reached the waistband of her jeans, she paused, darting out her tongue to catch a droplet of moisture which ran down his back. Moving her lips round, she transversed his waist, ending up near his navel. Paul sucked in his breath, hollowing his stomach as if in anticipation of the feel of her lips there and she moved away, teasing him.

She watched his face through half-closed eyes as she made her way up his chest to his nipples. Lathing one with the flat of her tongue, she fingered the other back to hardness. She loved the taste of the sensitive flesh, rolling the hard bud around her tongue until it swelled to what she guessed was the point of discomfort. Tilting her head back, she saw that the brown skin had turned a delicate shade of pinky-purple, rising and falling rapidly with his quickened breathing.

Turning her attention to the other side of his chest, she was careful to lavish as much time and attention on its twin. By the time she had finished, both nipples were standing erect and Paul's breathing was rapid and shallow.

Julia raised her head and scanned his face. His expression was curiously intent and standing still as she had requested was clearly becoming an effort of will. Pleased with him, she smiled and pressed a small kiss to the corner of his mouth.

'You are so, utterly gorgeous,' she praised him throatily. 'I could touch and kiss you all night long.'

He groaned and she chuckled gently. Putting out her tongue, she tickled it down his neck to the hollow where his collar bones joined. Here she paused to twirl it gently round and round, making him shudder.

Sinking to her knees on the carpet in front of him, she licked and kissed a path down his midline, swirling round his navel and burying her face in the soft mat of hair which protected his lower belly.

She could smell the sharp, heady scent of his arousal, could feel the sudden tightening of his stomach muscles as she rubbed her cheek against the straining bulge in his jeans. Leaning back on her heels, Julia looked up at him through eyes which had become heavy-lidded and glazy.

His face seemed a long way above her, his eyes roving appreciatively over the view of her breasts displayed to advantage in the cream silk bra. Stretching her spine, she paused briefly in the caresses to gather up her breasts in her hands, running her palms sensuously over the burgeoning nipples which showed darkly against the pale silk.

Paul let out his breath on a sigh.

'Let me. . .' he whispered, but Julia only smiled and shook her head.

'Plenty of time,' she murmured, turning her attention to the fastening of his jeans.

They had a button placket, the stiff buttonholes made even more difficult to negotiate by the pressure behind them. Slowly, patiently, Julia undid each one, revealing plain white cotton briefs which could barely contain his erection.

He trembled as she eased the stiff denim over his hips and pushed it down his legs. He reached down to pull his jeans off, removing his socks at the same time. Julia's attention was caught by his feet. Large, with straight white toes and neat nails. She stroked them, noticing how such a small gesture sent little shivers of delight up his legs.

His legs were sturdy, well-shaped with a dense covering of thick black hair, far more than was on his chest. Running her hands lightly up his calves, she described small, ticklish circles behind his knees before touching his thighs. They were rock-hard, hardly any flesh there to soften them, and Julia revelled in their wholly masculine texture, so different from her own fleshy thighs. She imagined them imprinting their shape on hers as they joined together, and relished the anticipation.

Her eyes flickered over his engorged shaft before she glanced upward again.

'I'm saving that for last,' she said mischievously. 'Right now I think I want you to turn around.'

He did so with obvious reluctance and Julia was faced with the sight of his taut, shapely buttocks level with her eyes. Giving in to the urge to cup and squeeze, she smiled at the way he instinctively tensed his muscles, creating two perfect dimples in the centre of each cheek.

Taking pity on him, for now at least, she reached up and hooked her fingers beneath the waistband of his briefs. With tantalising slowness, she rolled them down, over his hips, his thighs, his knees and calves, as if she was opening a present. He stepped out of them and kicked them to one side, apparently unselfconscious with his nakedness. He jumped as Julia pressed her lips against the point where his buttocks joined his legs and she hid a smile.

The time had come which she knew he had been waiting for. Putting her hands of his hips, she gently turned him so that he was facing her again. Her eyes widened as she came face to face with his engorged penis. He was very aroused; the skin was tight over his scrotal sac and the shaft itself was rigid, pointing straight upward from the thick nest of hair which surrounded the base.

With a sense of wonder, Julia ran her fingers lightly along the underside, fascinated to find that her touch made his cock twitch of its own accord.

'No,' he said hoarsely, 'I can't—'

'Yes you can,' she interrupted him firmly. 'You must. I don't want you to come yet – not before I've tasted you.'

Her words alone almost sent him over the edge and Julia hastily decided that it was now or never. She couldn't expect the poor man to withstand this kind of titillation indefinitely.

Remembering something she had read in a magazine, she pinched the circumscised helmet between her forefinger and thumb and, to her amazement, the immediate crisis seemed to pass. She liked the feel of him there; the skin was so soft, like fine velvet. Running her thumbnail lightly along the crease, she curled her fingers around the solid width of him and ran her hand up and down the shaft twice.

Paul was breathing heavily and his entire body was bathed in a fine film of perspiration. Julia could feel the heat of him from several inches away and she suddenly longed to draw that heat into her own body, to feel some of his vitality flowing through her veins.

Stretching her lips wide, she brought his cock-head to her mouth and enclosed him. The shudder seemed to vibrate right through him as, unable to stay still for a moment longer, he meshed his fingers in her hair. Fellatio had never been Julia's favourite activity. With Michael it was kept for when she really wanted to please him, so it was a rare occurrence these days. This time, though, with this young man whom she barely knew, Julia was mildly shocked to realise that there was nothing she desired more than to suck him.

Closing her eyes, she gripped him by the buttocks and pulled him closer to her, urging him to deepen his strokes until she could feel the muscles of her throat opening to accommodate him. Reaching between his legs, she cupped his balls with one hand and squeezed gently.

'Wait . . . I'm going to . . . I can't. . .' he gasped incoherently as he tried to withdraw from her mouth.

Julia held on to him, signalling her willingness, no, her *need* to see this through to the inevitable end. For a few seconds he seemed unable to comprehend that she intended to make him climax inside her mouth and he continued to try, frantically, to pull away. Then, with a groan of ecstatic defeat, he thrust into her one last time and Julia felt the hot, viscous emission hit the back of her throat.

She gulped as it seemed to go on and on, her lips milking him until his knees sagged and he sank down on to the floor in front of her. He was almost in tears, his breath coming in brief, sighing gasps as he sought to control himself.

'My God,' he gasped sliding his hands under

47

her hair and cupping her face, 'I can't believe you did that . . . I never dreamed. . .'

'Hush,' she whispered, 'and kiss me.'

He did, his lips seeking hers and his arms coming about her, crushing her to him. There was so much passion in that one kiss that Julia felt her own desire flare up and gather momentum. A kaleidoscope of the images imprinted in her mind whirled in her head, all of them powerfully erotic. She was glad when Paul, his strength quickly restored, took control. Sliding his arms around her shoulders and under her knees, he lifted her effortlessly on to the big, soft bed.

Exhausted by her own exertions, Julia lay back and allowed herself to succumb to sensation as he undressed her. There was a brief, painful moment of self-consciousness as she realised he was gazing down at her naked form. Then she saw the unstinting admiration in his eyes and she relaxed. After all, the light was dim and if he wasn't put off by the ravages of time which showed on her body, then she was determined that she would not be either!

Raising her arms above her head, she stretched, like a cat, aware of his eyes following the play of muscle and skin as her breasts were brought into soft relief.

Paul climbed on to the bed and straddled her, one knee either side of her thighs. Bending over her, he kissed her slowly, as she had him, from the base of her throat to one tender peak. Julia gasped as one hardening nipple was drawn into the hot, wet warmth of his mouth and he suckled gently on it. As if there was some invisible cord connecting her breasts to her sex, she felt an answering pull deep in her womb and her innermost flesh grew heavy and moist.

She moaned softly as he transferred his attention to her other breast, while his hands began a gentle exploration of her lower body. Julia sensed that he wanted to take as much time as she had, but that somehow his intentions and his actions could not quite combine. He tried to pay attention to her legs, her waist and belly, her arms and neck, but in the event these only received the briefest of caresses before he zeroed in on her breasts and sex.

It didn't matter. By this time, Julia was so aroused she would hardly have cared if there had been no preliminaries at all. When he delved clumsily into the soft, warm flesh between her thighs, she reached down and covered his hands with hers. Guiding him to the right spot, she showed him by her actions the right speed and pressure to make her sex-lips open out and enclose his fingers.

'Don't stop,' she murmured when his rhythm faltered as she took her hand away, 'I'm so close . . . oh!'

And indeed she was close, closer than she would have dreamed possible, to reaching the peak. Closing her eyes, she concentrated on the sensations building inside her, focusing on the tiny scrap of flesh which had hardened to a quivering mass of nerve endings which writhed beneath his fingers.

Bright flashes of colour flew across the insides of her eyelids as the familiar warmth suffused her, making her limbs heavy and her head swim. Suddenly everything seemed to explode in her brain and she cried out, scissoring her legs to trap Paul's hand for a moment as he pressed on her throbbing clitoris.

It was several moments before Julia could catch her breath enough to open her eyes and smile. Paul smiled back and she saw her own satisfaction mirrored in the dark blue of his eys. Content for now, she snuggled into his arms and closed her eyes the better to appreciate the warm, post-orgasmic glow which enveloped them.

After a few minutes, she stirred and eased herself away from him. Paul must have fallen into a light doze, for he sat up with a jerk, rubbing his hands over his face as he watched her pull on her clothes.

'You're going?'

Julia smiled at his startled expression.

'It's late.'

'I thought . . . I hoped. . .'

'I know. Did it matter to you that we didn't . . . you know . . . together?' she faltered, aware that, having shared such intimacy with him, it was ridiculous to feel shy now. He understood what she meant though and he shook his head.

'No. It was . . . it was beautiful. *You* are beautiful.'

Julia smiled, pleased with the simple compliment.

'Thank you. Don't get up, Paul. I noticed you have a phone – can I use it to ring for a taxi?'

He shot her a dark look and leaped out of bed.

'I'll do it for you,' he said, disappearing into the living-room.

Julia watched him, enjoying the sight of his naked, healthy body as he moved around the room. He was so unselfconscious, so at ease with his own body, Julia envied him. Once the taxi had been ordered, he came back into the bedroom and pulled on a fresh pair of jeans. Coming round to her, he kissed her lightly on the lips.

'Will I see you again?'

Julia looked up into his handsome face and was sorely tempted. Regretfully, she shook her head.

'I don't think so.'

'Why not?' He looked hurt.

Moving away from him slightly, Julia tried to explain.

'We don't know anything about each other, Paul, and I want to keep it that way. Tonight was . . . well, I don't usually do this sort of thing. But I know that tonight was special.'

Glancing across at him, she saw that his face had taken on a slightly sulky expression. It made him look very, very young and she bit her lip.

'It was just sex then, was it?' he said, pouting.

Julia thought of the pleasure she had shared with him and realised that she was taking away from this little flat much more than just a pleasant memory. He didn't know it, but in a few short hours, Paul had helped her recover her sense of herself as a woman. When he had seen her on the dance floor, he hadn't recognised the wife in her, or the mother. He had seen a sexy, desirable woman and that meant a very great deal to her.

'No,' she said softly, 'it wasn't just sex.' Leaning across the bed where he was now sitting, she kissed him gently on the cheek. 'It was far, far more than that.'

Seeing the confusion in his eyes, she smiled at him one last time, then she walked quickly out of the flat and went downstairs to wait for her taxi.

Chapter Four

THE LUNCHTIME RUSH on Monday at the coffee shop was almost over by the time Julia managed to grab a sandwich for herself. She rarely did get to eat before two-thirty and normally she was ravenous. Today though, she could hardly face the chicken and mayonnaise roll she had put by.

'Look at her – lovestruck!' Carolyn laughed as she and Sally came to sit down beside her.

Julia stretched her lips around a smile. She had hoped that because the day after Ann's hen-night had been her day off last week, by the time Monday came around the girls would have forgotten her disappearance on Thursday night. No chance – Carolyn hadn't stopped ribbing her since the moment she had walked in and she had to admit that the jokes were beginning to wear a bit thin.

Sally, the quieter of the two was looking at her thoughtfully, concern showing in her lovely grey eyes.

'Is there something wrong, Julia? Only you

don't seem yourself today.'

'Maybe lover boy wasn't up to scratch!' Carolyn guffawed and Sally frowned at her.

'I think that's a customer coming in, Caro,' she said pointedly, nodding towards the door.

Sure enough, another student from the nearby college was eyeing their depleted stock mournfully through the window. Carolyn glanced at her untouched sandwich and grimaced at the other two.

'I'll get it then, shall I?' she muttered ungraciously.

Sally waited until she was out of earshot before turning back to Julia.

'We could manage now if you want to go home early,' she suggested quietly.

Julia gave her a grateful smile.

'I'm fine, Sally, honestly. Just a little trouble at home – nothing that won't sort itself out. I'll go and start the clearing up, I think.'

A little trouble at home she repeated bitterly to herself as she filled the sink with hot, soapy water. After she had left Paul's flat, the guilt had begun to worm its way into her consciousness, so that by the time she arrived home she was feeling awful, wondering how she was going to look Michael in the eye at the breakfast table the following morning.

She needn't have worried. Michael wasn't at the breakfast table – in fact, he never came home at all that night. Melissa had been though and confronting her baleful, accusing stare was almost as bad as facing Michael.

'Where's your father?' Julia asked her, knowing

that Michael might well have said something about where he was going to their daughter.

'Dunno,' Melissa replied through a mouthful of cornflakes. 'Where were you until two o'clock this morning?'

Something about her tone made Julia's hackles rise.

'At a nightclub, as you well know. Why, were you waiting up for me?'

'Don't you think it was a bit late?'

'What I do is none of your business, young lady. At least I wasn't out all night!' she had snapped, wincing as Melissa predictably flounced out of the room, slamming the door behind her.

Michael had been shifty when he finally arrived in time for the *Big Match* on TV.

'You've been with *her*, haven't you?' Julia had held her breath, wanting him to deny it, yet knowing that he wouldn't. Somehow knowing that Michael had slept with Gail Jones again, after it was supposed to be all over between them, made her own indiscretion seem small and insignificant. 'When did that start up again – the night of our anniversary party? Or hadn't it ever really ended?'

Julia began to scrub the utensils with unnecessary vigour as she recalled how Michael had refused to discuss it with her. As if it had nothing to do with her at all. The atmosphere at home over the rest of the weekend had been unbearable and Julia wasn't sure how much more of it she could stand.

'Julia – someone to see you!' Carolyn's voice calling her from the front of the shop snapped her out of her gloomy reverie. 'You certainly like them young, don't you?' Carolyn said, *sotto voce*, as she came through.

Julia paused, towel in hand as she met the calm grey eyes watching for her appearance in the doorway.

'Nick!' Ignoring the way her heart seemed to skip a beat, Julia smiled and put down the towel. 'What are you doing here?'

'I thought I'd come and see how you ran things here. Any chance of a coffee and a sandwich?'

'I should think so – anything in particular?'

He smiled cheekily at her.

'Surprise me.'

Julia watched him surreptitiously out of the corner of her eye as she put together a hotchpotch of a sandwich from what was left. He was wearing worn-looking denim jeans with a faded orange sweatshirt. A battered denim jacket was slung over the back of his chair as he folded his long legs under the table and pushed the strands of dark blond hair which had escaped from his ponytail out of his eyes.

'I have to hand it to you, Julia – you've got great taste!' Carolyn murmured.

'For goodness' sake,' Julia replied, embarrassment sharpening her tone, 'he's a friend of Gavin's.'

'Mmm. Well ask that gorgeous son of yours if he's got a spare friend for me too, will you?'

Nick looked up as she approached with his sandwich and smiled at her.

'Will you have a cup of coffee with me?'

'Well, I really should be—'

'It's okay, Julia – Sally and I can finish up here,' Carolyn cut in gaily, bringing over two cups with the coffee pot. As she put them on the table she winked and Julia felt her face burn.

'I'm sorry about that!' she said quietly, seeing the amusement sparkling in the calm grey eyes watching her. 'Carolyn isn't known for her subtlety.'

'Does it bother you, being seen with me?'

'No,' she said, looking up at him in surprise. 'Should it?'

He smiled, rather enigmatically, Julia thought.

'I've brought you the prospectus from the college.' He took a thick brown envelope out of his rucksack and passed it over to her. Their fingers touched as she took it and the tip of his forefinger stroked the back of her hand in a brief caress.

Julia kept her gaze trained downwards so that he wouldn't see the sudden, shocking jolt of desire which his touch had triggered. What was the matter with her? Since her encounter with Paul her body seemed determined to anticipate erotic adventure with every personable man with whom she came into contact. Impatient with herself, she shifted in her seat and forced herself to listen to what he was saying.

'The course was undersubscribed this year so there are still one or two places left. I thought maybe you'd like to come and have a look round. See if it's what you really want.'

Julia felt cornered. Damn Gavin and the self-improvement plan he'd mapped out for her!

'That's just it, Nick,' she said, aware that her

voice was cracking slightly, 'I'm not sure that it is what I want. I mean, the coffee shop is okay—'

'Do you get to cook?'

'Not as much as I'd like,' she admitted reluctantly. God, she must sound so weak! Gavin had obviously sold the idea to Nick that she was raring to go, that she couldn't wait to go back to college and make a fresh start in life. What must he think of her now that she was sitting here prevaricating?

Aware that Nick was watching her closely over the rim of his coffee cup, she grimaced.

'You must think me very rude! It's very kind of you to bring me the prospectus and offer to show me round.'

'Not at all – it'll be my pleasure.'

There was something about the way he said the last words that made Julia glance up at him. His eyes had darkened to a deep, smoky grey and there was an expression in them which made another dart of awareness ricochet through her. Gradually, she realised his lower leg was pressing gently against hers, felt the warmth of his skin through the thick fabric of his jeans. It wasn't her imagination, he *was* flirting with her.

Briefly, she considered the possibilities. She liked the way he flattered her, unwittingly pouring balm on her wounded ego. Physically she found him very attractive, compelling almost. Was she being ridiculous? Nick was a friend of her son's, trying to do her a favour. It was silly to read anything more into it, foolish to feel so . . . excited. And yet his eyes held such a wealth of erotic promise. . .

'I'll tell you what,' she told him briskly in an attempt to bring things under control, 'why don't you and Gavin come for dinner tomorrow night? That'll give me a chance to read through the prospectus properly and you'll be able to give me your opinion on my cooking.'

The expression in his eyes told her that he knew what she was doing and he was amused by it. He put down his coffee cup and Julia blinked in surprise as she realised that he had eaten the sandwich while they had been talking.

'I'll look forward to it,' he said, scraping back his chair. 'If that sandwich was anything to go by it'll be cordon bleu.'

They both laughed and the tension between them evaporated.

'I'll see you tomorrow,' he told her.

'Yes. Bye.' She forced herself to not watch him as he walked out of the coffee shop.

'What's cooking, Mum?' Melissa asked, sniffing as she walked through the door.

'Swordfish steaks,' Julia told her, never taking her eyes off the pot. 'I've tried this recipe out on you before.'

'Not again! There's enough in there to feed an army. You look nice,' Melissa remarked suddenly, eyeing Julia's neat, pleated skirt and white blouse with approval.

'Like a mum is supposed to look?' Julia turned to face her.

'Well . . . yes, I suppose so.'

'Good. Gavin is coming to dinner tonight and bringing a friend with him.'

'Huh – you never invite Spider to dinner.'

'I hadn't realised Spider could use a knife and fork. Go and clean up now, they'll be here in half an hour.'

Once the door had slammed shut behind Melissa, Julia reopened it quietly and checked her appearance in the full-length mirror in the hall. She did look mumsy, she noted with satisfaction. She'd even put up her hair and put on the neat pearl clip earrings that her mother had given her for her last birthday.

If Nick had been under any misapprehension regarding her feelings towards him, this should scupper them! Attractive though he undoubtedly was, she had a feeling that he would not be content with the short-term fling she had offered Paul. And, while she knew that she was ripe for adventure, she couldn't handle anything more complicated than a one-night stand until she had sorted things out with Michael. Besides, Nick was Gavin's friend. It struck Julia as being a little . . . *unseemly* to allow the attraction that seemed to have flared between them to grow. She smiled to herself at the old-fashioned word, jumping as the doorbell rang and she saw the two figures behind the frosted glass. Taking a deep breath, she smoothed down her skirt and, fixing a smile on her face, she opened the door.

'Hi!' Gavin took in her appearance and his eyes registered his dismay.

Julia noticed the way Nick's unrestrained, wavy blond hair tumbled enticingly over his shoulders and clenched her fingers into fists to quell the impulse to run them through it.

'Hello Gavin – Nick. Come on in, dinner's almost ready.'

'You're looking very lovely tonight, Julia,' Nick said, his voice crackling with amusement.

He was looking at the demurely fastened buttons at her collar bone and Julia had the uncomfortable feeling that he was picturing himself undoing them. The hallway suddenly seemed far too narrow and she pressed herself against the wall. Opening her mouth to tell him to follow Gavin through to the living-room, she stopped as she saw his eyes were lingering on her parted lips.

'Nick. . .?' she whispered.

His eyes rose to meet hers and he smiled gently at her.

'I know what you're doing and it won't work. You won't put me off, you know,' he said softly.

'Why?' It was a foolish thing to say but the word seemed simply to spring to her lips before she could check it.

'Because you're quite the most exciting woman I've met for a long time.'

His voice was low and husky and Julia gradually became aware of the faint scent of his aftershave. He was standing so close to her that she could feel the warmth of him, could see every pore of his skin, smell the sweet, honeyed scent of his breath. She swayed slightly towards him, tempted to run the tip of her tongue along the inside of his lower lip, but she pulled back just in time.

Smiling, she said softly, 'Go through to the dining-room, Nick, and I'll serve dinner.'

When she walked in carrying the fish, Julia saw that Melissa had homed in on Nick and was hanging on to his every word. Nick looked up as she entered and his eyes widened appreciatively.

'That smells good.'

Julia smiled blandly and handed round the plates, looking up in surprise as the front door opened and Michael walked through.

'Michael! I wasn't expecting you – have you eaten?'

'Yes,' he replied tersely, his dark eyes taking in the scene in the dining-room. 'Gavin.' He nodded at his son, as if he felt duty-bound to acknowledge his visit, but his manners did not extend to Melissa or Nick. Julia watched in amazement as he dumped his briefcase on the hall table and disappeared upstairs without so much as another word.

It wasn't like Michael to be so moody and she instantly wondered what could have happened at work. Conscious that Nick was watching her, she shrugged and took her place at the table. Whatever was bothering Michael would simply have to wait until later.

Throughout the meal, Nick was solicitous towards Melissa, asking her about her college place and taking an interest in her search for digs.

'Actually, the reason I came tonight was to try to persuade your mother to take a catering course,' he said finally.

Melissa spluttered into her lemon sorbet and looked at Julia with open amusement.

'Mum? What would *she* want to go to college for?'

'Why shouldn't she do something new, Mel?' Gavin replied mildly when Julia didn't respond. 'After all, she's spent the last twenty years bringing us up.'

'Yeah.' Melissa looked uncomfortable. 'But *Mum* – at *college*?'

'I think Julia would enjoy the course,' Nick supplied helpfully.

By this time Julia decided she had had enough.

'When you've all quite finished discussing me as if I'm not here, perhaps you'd be good enough to pass your plates? Thank you. Now I'm off to the kitchen, Melissa, where you so clearly think I belong, where I'll stack the dishwasher.' Feeling miffed, she retreated from the silence which greeted her outburst.

As she clattered the dishes carelessly into the washer, she felt rather than saw someone come in. She knew without turning around that it was Nick.

'I'm sorry about that,' he said quietly. 'I hadn't meant for you to be upset.'

'I'm not upset!' she ground out through gritted teeth.

'No? I don't see why not – you have every right to be.'

Julia straightened and turned slowly to face him.

'Nick, it's very kind of you, I'm sure, but there's no need to humour the old girl! You stick to your own generation.'

'Why?'

Julia waved a tea towel at him in exasperation.

'Because although your attention is very

63

flattering, you must see that I'm far too old for you.'

'Do you think so?' He raised one dark blond eyebrow and leaned against the kitchen door as if settling in for a long discussion. Julia lost patience.

'Yes I do. Now why don't you bright young things take yourselves off out to where bright young things go in the evenings these days and leave me to deal with my moody husband?'

'Why don't you come with us?'

Julia missed a beat, then she laughed.

'Don't you ever give up?'

'No.'

'Well, this time you're going to have to.'

'We'll see,' Nick said softly and Julia was hard-pressed to conceal a shiver of anticipation.

'Let's go back to the others,' she said quietly.

In the end Melissa announced that she was meeting Spider and Gavin and Nick left Julia alone. Michael had emerged from the bedroom and could be heard resentfully making himself a cup of tea. Julia waited until the house was quiet before joining him in the kitchen.

'Did you make a pot?' she asked mildly, knowing full well that Michael would have used a single tea bag in a mug, never thinking to offer to make Julia a drink as well.

'The kettle's still warm,' he replied grudgingly.

Julia went over to it and turned it back on, watching Michael from the corner of her eye as she did so. His hair was still damp from the shower, his scalp showing pinkly on the top of his head. His boyish handsomeness, like his hair, was thinning now and Julia felt a pang of something like pity when she realised how worn-out he looked.

'Well? Are you going to tell me what's troubling you?' she asked him gently, reaching in the cupboard for a mug.

'I've told Gail it's over between us,' he blurted without warning.

Luckily Julia had her back to him, so he couldn't see her expression.

'Really?' she said with a calmness she was far from feeling. What did he expect her to say? Did he want her to be grateful?

'Yes. I thought it was best, considering the atmosphere in the house this past week . . . Well, anyway – it's been a long day. Are you coming to bed?'

Julia turned slowly to face him. He was eyeing her resentfully, blaming her, no doubt, for the ending of his relationship. Expecting her to leap gratefully into bed beside him. Her earlier pity gave way to cold contempt. Why did he take it for granted that she still wanted him? Did he think she saw him as a prize?

'All right,' she said, her voice dangerously soft.

Michael spent an age in the bathroom. When he came out, he was neatly pyjama'd, his hair was combed and, as he climbed into bed beside her, Julia caught the strong scent of toothpaste on his breath. She tensed as he switched off the lamp and put his hand heavily on her thigh, angry that he expected her to welcome his touch.

'I know it hasn't been easy for you,' he said unexpectedly in the darkness. 'I mean . . . you might not have realised, but it's always been the main thing, for me, you know . . . our marriage'

Julia's lips tightened.

'Really?' she drawled ironically. 'So you were thinking of me and our marriage, were you, when you were shagging Gail?'

Michael snatched his hand away from her leg as if the feel of her skin was suddenly repellent to him.

'Jesus Christ, Julia – do you have to be that crude? I've said I'm sorry and I've broken things off with Gail. What more do you want?'

Julia lay silent for a while, seething quietly to herself.

'*I* slept with someone else.'

From the way Michael jumped as she spoke, she guessed he had been on the verge of sleep.

'What's that?'

'I said I slept with someone else. The other night, the night of Ann's hen-party – I picked up a young man in a nightclub and went back to his flat.'

Michael sighed heavily.

'Don't be childish, Julia,' he said wearily.

Julia smiled in the darkness. She had known he wouldn't believe her, but had wanted the satisfaction of knowing that she, at least, had been honest. Suddenly she was gripped by an overwhelming urge to remind him of what he had thrown away all these years when he had chosen Gail over her.

'Michael?'

'Hmm?'

'Was she good in bed? Oh that was a stupid

question – of course she was or you wouldn't have kept on going back for more, would you?'

'Julia—' Michael began, warningly, but Julia cut him off.

'I like sex – did you know that?. I *like* to feel a man's mouth at my breasts, to feel strong fingers between my legs. . .'

'Julia! What's got into you. . .?'

She ignored him.

'I *like* being licked and sucked down there and I *like* drawing a thick, hard cock inside my body and milking it dry—'

'Julia!'

'What's the matter? Don't you like to hear me talk like this?' Her fingers crept across the front of his pyjama trousers and she felt the heat of his erection. 'Shame on you, Michael – I do believe you like it after all!'

She silenced him then by rolling over so that she was pinning him down with the upper part of her body and crushing his mouth under hers. He tasted so familiar. The hands which gripped her waist had fondled her so many times over the years, Julia had thought there could be no surprises between them any more. Never before, though, had she felt the need to subjugate him like this, to punish him, and the new feeling swamped her, making her dizzy with desire.

A groan vibrated in the back of Michael's throat and Julia broke away from him, feeling triumphant. Her fingers working with feverish anger at the buttons of his pyjamas, she stripped him, noticing as she did so that his penis was already semi-hard, rising up in unsuspecting anticipation.

Julia felt hot now. She tore at her own nightclothes, ignoring Michael's look of wary excitement as her nakedness was revealed. She could sense that, while his body was undeniably aroused by her initiative, mentally he wasn't quite sure what to make of it. Smiling to herself, she wondered if he was afraid that she had hidden the sewing scissors in her bedside drawer, or had devised some other torture for him. Oh no, that would be too brutal, far less satisfying than what she had in mind.

Smiling, Julia bent her head and allowed her long, soft hair to trail across the smooth, almost hair-free planes of his chest. Michael moaned, swallowing hard as it brushed across the sensitive skin of his glans.

'Julia. . .'

This time when he said her name it was more of a plea than a reprimand and Julia knew she had him where she wanted him. It was so sweet to know that, while she took her pleasure from him he was blissfully unaware that it would be the last time. She had already decided that tomorrow she would leave him.

Briefly, as she dipped her head to take one of his responsive nipples between her lips, she wondered, why now? Why had she decided enough was enough just as he had announced that he was leaving Gail? Perhaps it was the way he had expected her to be grateful that he had decided to put her first, at last, she mused as she lathed the other nipple with her tongue.

Michael's hands clutched convulsively at her waist before plucking feverishly at her dangling breasts. Julia moved out of his range, determined that, this last time, she would be the one who was in charge. Straddling him, she took his straining cock between her palms and moved them up and down the silky skin of the shaft. Michael's breath rasped in his throat as the exposed glans began to moisten with the clear seepage of pre-emission and Julia bent over him, thrusting one succulent breast into his willing mouth.

Rolling her nipple on his tongue, Michael groped for the soft, hot flesh between her legs, groaning as she knocked him away with her hands.

'Lie still!' she hissed, and, although he barely recognised this side of his wife, he automatically responded to the note of command in her voice.

Julia began to stimulate herself, moving her hips back and forth along his thigh so that the sensitive inner folds of her vulva were stimulated by the harsh rasp of his body hair. His flesh grew slick with her juices, shining in the pale shaft of moonlight which crept through a gap in the curtains.

To her surprise, what had started out as a desire to provoke and subdue him soon became secondary to her own need for release. She felt hot all over, the familiar, churning warmth radiating out from her belly into her limbs, making her feel weak, yet powerful all at once. Michael had his eyes closed and she could tell from the shallowness of his breathing and the intense look of concentration on his face that he was about to come.

Frustrated with the lack of finesse involved in

masturbating herself against his leg, Julia transferred her right hand to her own needy sex and quickly brought herself to the point of crisis. Stimulating Michael became an automatic process as she was suddenly, unexpectedly assailed by the memory of Nick's calm grey eyes as they had swept over her in the kitchen.

'You are quite the most exciting woman I have met in a long time,' he had told her.

And I am! she thought fiercely. The poor bastard now gasping for release beneath her just didn't have the wit to realise it! She came just before he did, gritting her teeth to cage the name of the young man who had aroused her far more by a look, a few soft words than the man now caught in the throes of orgasm beneath her.

In the split second after she came, Julia recognised how much she wanted Nick, and how little she wanted her husband. But that did not lessen her anger when Michael opened his eyes and smiled at her.

'I knew I'd made the right decision,' he told her.

Julia could not stomach his smugness, could not bear him at all and she lay down, turning her back towards him.

'So have I,' she whispered to herself, clutching her secret to her like a security blanket.

Michael got up and went to the bathroom before slipping back into bed, naked, beside her. Julia shrugged off the arm he lay across her and he turned over, accepting the rejection without a murmur. Within minutes he was asleep.

Julia lay awake, listening to his soft snores. He

always slept soundly after sex, so much so that she had often thought he would sleep through fire and enemy attack without so much as stirring. She wondered now why she had stayed for so long. Habit, she supposed, and, of course, there had been the children to consider. Now, though, Gavin was settled in his own flat and Melissa would be leaving for college at the weekend. She couldn't use the children as a shield to hide behind any more. There was no longer anything to keep her here.

Julia was looking forward to seeing the smugness slip off Michael's face when she told him in the morning that she was leaving him. She wondered if Gail would be willing to take him back? She was welcome to him, yet it seemed a shame not to leave them both something to remember her by. Suddenly her eyes fell on the indelible marker pen on the bedside table which she had been using earlier to mark Melissa's belongings ready for her departure.

Julia smiled wickedly. She couldn't. She wouldn't. Grabbing the pen, she uncapped it and slipped out of bed. Going round to Michael's side of the bed, she slowly peeled the covers away from his torso until his penis, soft and sated now, came into view. Picking it up between her forefinger and thumb, she stretched it out gently, holding it still as she wrote her name in block capitals on the soft, wrinkled skin. Stepping back to admire her handiwork, Julia pictured Gail's reaction when she saw Michael's new 'tattoo'. When he was erect, 'JULIA' would be emblazoned along the length of his penis like a declaration of his infidelity. Stifling a giggle, Julia went back to her own side of the bed where she fell quickly into a deep, dreamless sleep.

The following morning Julia was downstairs clearing away the breakfast dishes when she heard the yell from the bathroom. She smiled to herself as Michael appeared, red-faced and incredulous at the doorway.

'How *could* you, Julia?'

She turned to face him, wiping her hands on the tea towel and folding it carefully over the radiator to dry.

'It was my pleasure!' Taking pity on him she shrugged. 'It'll wear off, Michael – eventually!'

'But I thought . . . last night . . . for God's sake, Julia! I thought that last night. . .' He seemed incapable, suddenly, of finishing a sentence.

'Poor Michael! You don't get it, do you? Last night meant nothing, nothing at all, not after what you've put me through. I'm leaving you, Michael.'

'Leaving. . .? When?'

'I thought I'd wait until Melissa has moved out – that'll give us both time to settle the details—'

'What details.' Michael was spluttering, clearly unable to take everything in.

'Selling the house—'

'Why?'

'Well, I certainly don't want to live here alone, and I expect that you'll move in with Gail, won't you? She has a house of her own, doesn't she?'

'I told you – it's all over between Gail and me.'

Julia shrugged.

'That's your problem, Michael. All *I* know is that it's all over between you and me.'

Michael still seemed stunned, looking at her as if she'd suddenly started speaking Chinese.

'But last night. . .?'

'Last night, my dear, was nothing more than a farewell fuck.'

Flashing him an overbright smile, Julia turned and walked out of the back door. She was still chuckling to herself over Michael's stunned expression when she arrived to open up the coffee shop.

Chapter Five

JULIA WAS AMAZED at how quickly she was able to turn her whole life upside-down. One minute, it seemed, she was settled into a twenty-year-old marriage with a safe, if terminally dull, routine; the next she was moving into the flat Carolyn had told her about.

Gavin and Nick helpd her to move in, using the van Nick ran to carry his disco equipment to and from venues. Fenella Learman, her new landlady, greeted them on the doorstep with a huge, welcoming grin.

'Can't stop – as you can see, I'm right in the middle of something,' she said briskly, reaching into the voluminous pockets of her paint-splattered artist's smock for the keys. 'Give me a call if there's anything you need!' With that she disappeared into the back room which, Julia had learned, had been converted to a studio.

'She seems like quite a character,' Gavin whispered.

'Ssh – she'll hear you! Actually I've seen her

work – it's very good, as far as I can tell.'

The flat was really the top floor of a crumbling Victorian terrace. It could only be reached via the stairs of the main house, which Julia felt might prove to be a drawback. Fenella Learman, though, did not strike her as being the sort who would not respect her privacy, provided Julia did likewise and, besides, the rent was very reasonable.

'Christ, Ma – how many stairs are there?' Gavin puffed as he carried a boxful of books up yet another flight.

'You're out of condition!' Julia laughed, turning her new key in the door and throwing it open. 'Here – what do you think?'

The two men put down what they were carrying with visible relief and straightened up together. The door opened directly into the main room which, like all of the flat, was high-ceilinged with the original architraves and dado rails still intact. The walls had been painted a bright, sunny yellow and the paintwork had recently been given a fresh coat of brilliant white gloss. A faint trace of paint could still be detected hanging in the air, mingling with the slightly musty smell of the old velvet curtains framing the tall sash window on the opposite wall. They must once have been a dark green, but over the years they had been bleached by the sun so that they were now a lighter, more springlike shade which sat quite happily with the rest of the colour scheme.

'It's . . . big!' Gavin exclaimed, pushing the box of books over to the far wall where a pine bookshelf stood empty and waiting.

Julia laughed, pleased with his approval.

'The bedroom's not much smaller and there's a kitchen and bathroom at the back.'

Nick caught her eye and smiled at her.

'Looks like you've fallen on your feet,' he remarked as Gavin ran downstairs to fetch another box.

'It does rather, doesn't it?' Julia hugged herself, looking round the bright and airy room with satisfaction.

'Let me take you out to celebrate.'

'Now Nick—'

'What's stopping you? You've left Michael, you're a free agent – or is it simply that you don't want to come out with me?'

'You know it isn't that.'

'Do I? Look, what's wrong with two friends sharing a meal together? I'll even let you pay and call it a favour for hauling all your stuff up here!'

Put like that, Julia felt it would be churlish to refuse.

'Okay. We'll ask Gavin as well, shall we?' She laughed as Nick rolled his eyes at her. 'It's only fair – he's helped too.'

'Who's helped too?' Gavin gasped, staggering in with a suitcase. 'From where I'm standing I'd say I've done the bulk of the work!'

Julia and Nick both laughed and Nick, taking the rather heavy hint, left to fetch more cases.

'I was saying that I'd take you both for a meal tonight to say "thank you",' Julia explained.

'Oh Ma, can I take a rain check on that?'

'Hot date?'

To her surprise, Gavin's cheeks reddened slightly.

'You could say that. Why don't you take Nick by himself?'

Julia glanced at him worriedly.

'You wouldn't mind?'

Gavin shook his head.

'Have some fun, Mum. You deserve it.'

'But . . . Nick's your friend. . .'

'I'd far rather my mother was dating someone I know. You weren't planning on becoming celibate, were you?' he said when she raised her eyebrows at his casual mention of her new social status. 'He's crazy about you, Ma.'

Julia grimaced.

'Don't be silly!'

Gavin came over to her and put his arms around her shoulders.

'I just want you to be happy. Isn't that what all sons want for their mothers?'

Julia hugged him.

'Thanks Gavin – you don't know what it means to hear you say that. I just wish that daughters felt the same way!'

Gavin's mouth tightened as they both remembered the way Melissa had taken the news that her parents were separating. 'What about me?' she'd raged. 'How can you be so *selfish*. . .'

'She'll come round, you'll see.'

Julia wasn't so sure, but she kept her own counsel, turning to Nick as he reappeared in the doorway.

'Okay, Nicholas – you win. Where do you want to eat?'

He grinned.

'I know the perfect place. Can I use your phone

to book a table?'

'Be my guest.'

Both men stayed for a good hour, helping her to sort out her belongings and bring the flat into some semblance of order. When they finally left, with Nick promising to call for her at eight, Julia was left alone in her new home for the first time.

The silence was deafening. To her surprise, Julia found herself missing the chatter, the simple companionship of the other two almost at once.

'Don't be ridiculous!' she scolded herself. 'You'll soon get used to it.' The sound of her own voice bouncing off the walls was strangely disconcerting and she went to make herself a drink, banging around in the kitchen to cover the silence. She'd just settled herself in the saggy, comfortable, green chenille-covered sofa, when there was a knock at the door. The youth standing outside was tall and bespectacled, dark-haired and smooth-skinned, his cheeks unmarred by the slightest hint of beard.

'Hello!'

Julia smiled questioningly at him.

'Mrs Penn – Mum said to see if you've got everything you need,' he mumbled, carefully looking at a point slightly above her left collar-bone, as if too shy to meet her eyes.'

'Oh – you must be Greg! Would you like to come in?'

She stood aside, noticing the look of near-alarm which passed across his thin, intelligent-looking face.

'Er – no, I'm on my way out actually, Mrs Penn. Shall I say you're okay?'

'Yes, thanks, Greg. And please – call me Julia.'

He looked startled and his eyes flickered briefly to meet hers before darting away again. In that brief instant, Julia saw through his glasses that they were a clear, hyacinth blue, quite, quite beautiful.

'Um, right. Bye Mrs . . . Julia.'

'Bye Greg,' she said softly, watching as he loped back down the stairs, 'see you again soon.'

She soon forgot about him as she ran herself a bath and dressed ready for the evening ahead. When Nick rang her doorbell just after eight, she was feeling fresh and energetic in soft clean jeans and a linen shirt which she wore with large, dangly silver earrings and high-heeled boots.

'You're looking gorgeous!' he said, taking her by surprise and planting a kiss on her cheek.

'You're not so bad yourself!' she countered, moving smoothly away from him to fetch her bag.

Turning back to face him she saw that she was right, he really was looking rather . . . well . . . *gorgeous*! His dark blond hair was loose, rippling over his broad shoulders in shiny waves. A cream-coloured shirt was tucked into a pair of 501's which perfectly accentuated the long, lean length of his thighs. Julia's eyes lingered momentarily on the discreet silver buckle of his belt which rested against the flat planes of his stomach and he chuckled.

'Would you like me to walk to the door and back so that you can see me from all angles?'

Julia looked up, her eyebrows raising and laughed as she saw the amusement on his face.

'Was I staring?'

'A bit.'

She shrugged.

'Well, you know what men have been telling women for years – if you dress to impress then don't complain when you're ogled!'

'Ogled? Why Mrs Penn – were you *ogling* me?'

Julia laughed and moved pointedly to the door. When he didn't immediately follow her, she turned back and raised one quizzical eyebrow.

'I don't know about you, but I'm hungry!'

Nick smiled, a slow, wolfish smile which sent little shivers up and down her spine. For a moment she thought he was going to say something tired and clichéd like "hungry for what?" or whatever, but he did not disappoint her. Instead he simply strode to the door and held it open for her, waiting patiently while she locked it before allowing her to precede him down the stairs.

She raised her eyebrows when she saw he had brought the van. Catching her expression, Nick paused.

'What's the matter, Mrs Penn – did you expect a Merc?'

Julia was glad it was dark so that he couldn't see the flush of guilt on her cheeks.

'Of course not! I'm not a snob, Nick.'

He laughed.

'Everyone is, to a certain extent. You must remember, though, that I'm a student. I'm not ashamed of it – I won't be this poor for ever!'

'I'm sure you won't,' Julia murmured contritely as she slipped into the passenger seat. She noticed that he had covered the torn fabric with a blanket so that she would be comfortable and she felt ashamed for her initial dismay.

To her surprise, the restaurant turned out to be a small Italian trattoria on the edge of town. As soon as they stepped through the door, it seemed that all the waiting staff converged on them.

'Julia—' Nick said, extricating himself at last, 'I'd like you to meet my uncle, Guiseppe, and this is Pietro and Dommini.'

Julia found her hand being pumped enthusiastically as they were led to a corner table where they were seated with much ceremony and fussing about with linen napkins and cutlery.

'So,' Julia said when at last they were left alone, 'you're a dark horse! I must say, you don't *look* very Italian.'

Nick laughed.

'I know. I'm only half-Latin, but I always felt I missed out on the dark, mysterious good looks!' Giving a passable impression of a Valentino-style smoulder, he passed her the menu.

Julia smiled.

'Oh, I don't know – from where I'm sitting, I'd say that you did all right out of the deal.'

Nick raised an eyebrow at her but was prevented from replying by the return of Guiseppe who, snatching the menus from their hands, presented them with two steaming platters of spaghetti in a rich bolognese sauce.

'Good Lord, I'll never be able to eat all this!' Julia exclaimed.

'Better try,' Nick replied, picking up his fork. 'Guiseppe's bolognaise is his pride and joy!'

It was delicious, quite unlike any other common or garden spaghetti bolognese Julia had ever tasted. As they ate, washing down the food with a heavy Chianti, they talked and she found herself relaxing more and more.

'It was Uncle Guiseppe who first taught me how to cook,' Nick told her. 'He seems proud of me now, but, to be honest, I think he was a bit put out at first when I didn't automatically join him here after school.'

'Why didn't you?'

'I wanted to expand my knowledge – learn to cook all kinds of food.'

As Nick was driving, it was Julia who drank most of the Chianti. Enveloped in a warm, alcohol-induced glow, she smiled fondly at him.

'And not just spaghetti?'

'And not just spaghetti,' Nick conceded self-mockingly.

Julia smiled, liking him all the more for his honesty.

'What about the future – you graduate this year, don't you?'

He nodded.

'Yes. Initially, if I'm lucky, I'll find a post under a good chef.'

'And long-term?'

'I'd like a restaurant of my own. And I'm arrogant enough to want that sooner rather than later!'

'Maybe that's confidence, not arrogance. Don't be so hard on yourself!'

Nick laughed, absently tracing the pattern of the cloth with his fingertip for a few seconds.

'That's me all over, I suppose – when I see what I want I go for it, all the way, no compromise.'

He looked up suddenly and their eyes met

across the red-checked cloth. Julia caught her breath. In the smoky, flickering light of the candles he looked exquisitely desirable, his tranquil grey eyes almost guileless as he gazed at her. As she watched, the pupils widened and his lips parted, so slightly, and yet it was enough to make her realise that he too was suddenly finding it difficult to breathe.

On an impulse, Julia reached for his hand across the table. It was warm and dry, and she ran the pad of her thumb back and forth across the soft hairs on its back. Beneath the table, his calf pressed familiarly against her and the small, intimate contact sent a flicker of sensation up her leg.

Julia opened her mouth to say something, but her throat was too dry, her senses too dizzy and she could only watch as he slowly raised her hand to his lips. Her skin tingled as he gently unfolded her closed fingers and pressed his lips against each tip in turn before placing a small kiss in the centre of her palm. She shivered as her nipples hardened in response to the small stimulus and her womb contracted with longing.

To hell with the fact that Nick was a friend of her son, to hell with everything but this slow, delicious heaviness, trickling like warm honey through her limbs, making her want him.

'Let's go,' she whispered. Taking out her cheque book, she filled out a cheque and left it on the table. She was quite sure that the amount was adequate, but she didn't want to wait to check. She wanted to be home – now.

Some sixth sense, or Latin wisdom, prevented

his relatives from descending upon them again and they left the trattoria unimpeded. Nick unlocked the passenger door and held it open for her.

'Your place?' he asked her.

Julia nodded. She supposed it was all right – her new landlady hadn't presumed to make any rules about overnight guests.

Nick fired the engine and they drew away. Julia watched his hands on the steering wheel. They were strong, capable hands and she imagined how they would feel sliding across her skin, exploring the moist crevices of her most intimate flesh. . .

Leaning into him, she lay her head gently against him as they drove, absorbing the play of muscles in his shoulder as he changed gear. Neither broke the heavy, highly-charged atmosphere in the car for fear of disturbing the erotic spell keeping them in thrall. As far as Julia was concerned they couldn't get home soon enough.

By the time they arrived at the house, Julia was excited beyond belief, simply through imagining what the next few hours would hold. Perhaps it was the memory of her encounter with Paul, perhaps it was simply the thrill of the hitherto illicit, but she could not remember ever having felt so eager for sex.

Her fingers fumbled with the keys and she was glad when Nick's warm fingers covered hers and helped her guide the key into the keyhole. Looking back at him over her shoulder, she sucked in her breath as she saw the intensity in his eyes. Creeping through the door, she almost jumped out of her skin when Greg appeared in the drawing-room doorway. He blushed crimson when he saw her, his eyes flickering nervously from her to Nick and back again.

'Oh! Sorry, Mrs Penn . . . Julia . . . I thought it must be Mum . . . I . . . well, goodnight.' He retreated hastily and Julia felt sorry that she'd caused him embarrassment. She hesitated for a moment, wondering whether she should go to speak to him, but Nick was making use of the time she spent standing on the bottom step of the stairs to caress her bottom through the soft denim of her jeans and she quickly forgot Greg in the rapid spiral of desire which ran through her.

Nick began kissing her neck as she unlocked the door to her flat and they stumbled through it as one body. Kicking the door closed behind them, Nick turned her in his arms and pulled her closer to him.

'Alone at last!' he murmured wickedly in her ear and Julia smiled.

Her hands moved restlessly across the front of his shirt, wanting to feel the silky heat of his skin against her fingers. His chest was so warm, so hard, she had an overwhelming urge to press her softness against him, to feel her breasts flatten and swell against the enticingly hard slabs of muscle which divided his chest neatly in two.

Tugging at his shirt, she pulled it out of the waistband of his jeans and slipped her hands between the cool fabric and his hot skin. Closing her eyes, she ran her palms across his taut belly and up to his chest, revelling in the feel of his bare, firm flesh beneath her fingers. Her eyes flew open in surprise as his hands suddenly covered hers, stilling them.

'Not so fast.' He laughed at her, amused. 'We've got all night, haven't we?'

Smiling enigmatically at her, he led her by the hand into the bedroom. It was a large, square room with a double bed and an old-fashioned matching suite of furniture where Julia had hung her clothes earlier. Like the living-room, it had a tall sash window. The curtains were still tied back and the silvered beams of light from the full moon fell across the bed, obviating the need for artificial light.

Julia eyed Nick almost warily, unsure as to whether she liked the way he had taken charge. In the back of her mind she had supposed that, because he was so much younger than her, he would be happy to let her set the pace, just as Paul had.

'I want to look at you,' she whispered experimentally, reaching for his shirt buttons when he did not immediately react.

To her consternation, he actually chuckled.

'All in good time . . . let me kiss you. . .'

His hands cupped her head, holding her still while his lips teased the corner of her mouth, the tip of his tongue coaxing her lips apart. As if of their own volition, Julia felt her arms reach up to cling to him while her eyes fluttered restlessly to a close.

It wasn't so bad, relinquishing the control she had asserted, at least not while his hands were roaming the contours of her back, applying just the right amount of pressure to the small of her back while his tongue was plundering her mouth.

She was liquid, flowing into him, enclosing him as she sought to press her body closer to his. As the kiss went on she had no choice but to cling; her legs had turned to jelly, unable to support her. She was relieved when he lowered her gently onto the bed.

'Now I want to look at *you*,' he told her, stifling her murmur of protest with another kiss.

He started at the bottom, unlacing her right boot and slipping it off her foot, massaging her toes and the ball of her foot before removing her left boot. Julia gave in to the urge to stretch the muscles of her calf and foot and Nick bent to kiss the sensitive place behind her ankle bone.

Julia opened her eyes and looked up at him as he slowly stripped off her blouse, lifting her hips automatically as he eased her jeans down. His eyes flickered appreciatively over the soft apricot bra and brief set which was now the sole barrier between his eyes and her skin.

To her surprise, he didn't remove them immediately, rather he began to stroke the softly rounded contours of her stomach. Stretching himself out alongside her on the bed, he supported himself on one elbow, gazing down on her face and planting small, butterfly kisses around her hairline as he caressed her.

It was quite the most comforting feeling Julia had ever experienced, having her stomach stroked like this. And yet it did not detract from the eroticism of the moment, for as Nick caressed her rhythmically with the palm of his hand, the motion caused a referred pressure to be applied to the soft folds of flesh of her vulva.

She murmured slightly as she felt the labia moisten and expand, chafing against the silky underwear. Reaching up, she touched his hair, running it through her fingers and rubbing a hank of it against her cheek. It smelled of almonds and felt like a skein of silk rope. She imagined it sweeping across her naked skin and she shivered.

'Cold?' he asked her, frowning as his fingers brushed the goosebumps rising on her flesh.

Julia shook her head, not daring to speak in case she spoiled the mood of the moment. Nick smiled at her and dipped his head, pressing his lips against her navel. She jumped as she felt the pointed tip of his tongue delve wetly inside and he rubbed his cheek against the soft skin of her belly. His hair tickled her, making the goosebumps rise again and she reached down to run her fingers through the long tresses.

She could feel his warm breath whispering across her skin as he brushed his lips against the valley between her breasts before making his way with little, sucking kisses along her collar bone to her neck. Julia knew that her heartbeat had grown faster and she stirred restlessly as he pressed his lips against her racing pulse.

Supremely conscious that he was still fully-clothed while she was lying in her bra and pants, she plucked ineffectually at the buttons of his shirt. To her relief, he stood up and began to slip the buttons through the buttonholes. Julia slid up the bed and half sat up, leaning back against the pillows so that she could watch him as he stripped.

He was standing in a pool of moonlight which cast an eerie, silvery glow across his skin. Julia's eyes narrowed as he tossed the shirt aside and she admired the wholly masculine contours of his upper body. His muscle definition was just as she liked it; clear, but not excessively so. The veins fretting the insides of his arms looked strong, the thick blond hair growing along his arms and across his chest appeared to be soft, designed to be touched.

He held her eye as he began to slip his belt through the belt loops of his jeans. She could sense his tension from the way he held himself, with exaggerated poise, and she felt a fresh rush of moisture between her thighs. She loved this moment, when a men was teetering on the brink of arousal, still keeping it in check, yet barely so! The combination of potency and vulnerability was a powerful one and Julia always savoured the few seconds before lust won over self-control.

Nick's button fly was undone now and he hooked his thumbs in the twin waistbands of his jeans and his underpants so that they would both be removed together.

Julia held her breath as he stepped out of them, her eyes held by the sight of his long, slender penis which stood up from the nest of coarser hair below his belly. He was gratifyingly well-aroused, the circumcised tip of his cock glistening with the clear drop of moisture which had leaked from its end. Barely realising what she was doing, Julia ran the tip of her tongue along her lips. His cock twitched in response as he noticed the gesture and he came back to join her on the bed.

Without a word, he gathered up one breast in his hand and smoothed the lacy cup aside with his thumb. Julia's nipple sprang to life as his thumb pad brushed across it and he smiled at her, that enigmatic, wolfish smile which always turned her on. She gasped as he shifted position slightly, moving himself further up the bed so that he could press the tip of his penis against the hard rosy nub of her straining nipple, bathing it in the clear fluid which seeped from the slit.

'Oh . . . Nick?' She murmured an incoherent question as he began the stroking of her belly again while, with his cock, he played with her breast.

'You don't know how much I've wanted you,' he murmured huskily against her ear.

'Tell me,' she whispered, barely recognising her own voice.

'That first night – I saw you watching your husband dancing with another woman . . . I wanted to take you away, to hold you, to fuck you over and over until you didn't care any more. . .'

'Oh Nick, I wish you had!' Julia responded fervently, giving a little cry of distress as he slid his penis down her body.

He laughed softly.

'Then in the coffee shop . . . I can't tell you what I wanted to do with those cream buns and choux pastries. . .'

'Nick!' Julia laughed, wriggling her hips to encourage him to move his massaging fingers further down.

He didn't. Instead he lowered his head and nuzzled the front of her panties, inciting her to part her legs so that he could rub his nose against their damp crotch.

'Mmm, you're so hot down here . . . so sweet . . . I knew you would be!'

He raised his head and kissed her. Julia caught the heavy, honeyed scent of her feminine secretions on his lips and moved restlessly against his hand. He would not be rushed, though, he simply continued to massage her mound through the thin fabric of her panties. The pressure was building now in her clitoris and Julia knew that she would come at the first contact of his flesh with hers.

'When I came into the kitchen and you were stacking the dishwasher . . . do you know what a sight you present when you're bending over?'

Julia shook her head restlessly from side to side, wanting the low, intimate cadence of his voice to continue as much as she wanted the slow, steady rhythm of the heel of his hand against her pubis to keep going.

'Your skirt was stretched across your bottom so that I could see its shape . . . like a ripe, succulent peach. . .'

Behind her closed eyelids, Julia could see what he was describing, knew that she had tempted him all along, even when she hadn't meant to.

'I wanted to come up behind you and pull up your skirt . . . that modest, navy blue skirt that you were hiding behind. In my mind's eye I could see you weren't wearing anything underneath . . . so demure on the outside, yet so *hot* underneath! Oh Julia, I so wanted to put my hands on the soft halves of your buttocks and part them. . .'

Julia gasped at the images his words were conjuring up, and she was enveloped in a surge of heat so ,great that she felt the sweat begin to push through her pores.

'You wouldn't look at me, you'd simply put your hands flat on the open door of the dishwasher while I unzipped my fly . . . you'd be wet, of course, ready for me, and I'd plunge into you, skewer you against the kitchen work surface while my hands reached beneath you and squeezed your breasts. . .'

'Oh God, Nick . . . Nick please . . . next time . . . next time you see me like that. . .'

'I'll do it to you, Julia, I'll fuck you senseless, wherever, whenever you want me to—'

'Now? Will you do it now?' Her voice was urgent, feverish as she pushed ineffectually at the waistband of her panties.

Nick helped her, pulling the last barriers between them away from her body and throwing them on to the floor. As soon as her legs were freed, they opened, her swollen inner labia pouting wantonly through her outer lips, begging for his touch.

'Not now Julia,' he whispered throatily. 'Now I want to watch your face as you come. . .'

He touched her then, running the tip of his middle finger along first one channel, then the other before squeezing the two sides together so that her swollen clitoris was pushed out to its fullest extent. Then he flicked it, so lightly, with his thumb pad and at once Julia found herself falling, falling into a vortex of sensation.

She lost all control over her body. Her hips

bucked, her breasts thrust upward towards Nick's waiting mouth and she writhed beneath him. He sucked hard at the nipple he had caught between his lips while with his fingers he tapped firmly on the tiny point which, for now, seemed to be the very nerve centre of her body.

Julia could not prevent her ecstatic cries from bursting from between her lips as it went on and on, a kaleidoscope of colours whirling on the inside of her closed eyelids, making her head spin. She lost all sense of where she was, even who she was as sheer sensation blocked out every other impulse.

It was some minutes before she realised that Nick was cradling her in his arms. One hand was stroking soothingly across her twitching belly while the other smoothed the sweat-damp hair from her face. Slowly, she became aware that her pulse was slowing down, her body temperature was cooling and she could breath again, albeit shallowly.

Opening her eyes tentatively, she was glad that the light from the moon was a gentle light, for her eyes had expected a glare. Nick was gazing down at her, a look of wonder in his eyes.

'Are you all right?' he asked her when he saw the uncertainty in her eyes.

Was she all right? Julia felt a smile spreading across her face as she realised that she had just experienced the most amazing orgasm of her entire life. At that moment she loved him absolutely, knew that she would remember this night as the night she found out for the first time the heights to which she was capable of climbing.

'Of course,' she reassured him, reaching up to stroke his cheek. 'I feel fine ... let me show you. . .'

Ignoring the languor which had invaded her limbs, she rose up and straddled him, smiling as she saw his eyes widen with surprise.

'Let me see if I can make you feel the same way. . .'

Chapter Six

NICK'S BREATH HISSED between his lips in a small, shuddering sigh and he closed his eyes. Julia felt the tremor pass through him and was immediately re-aroused, her still-pulsing vulva opening to kiss the straining rod of his penis before sliding down his closed legs.

She admired his self-control. That he was teetering on the brink of climax was obvious from the shallowness of his breathing and the rigidity of his penis. Julia touched a finger lightly to his hair-roughened balls and marvelled at their tightness. Cupping them gently, she felt their weight and their heat and she stroked them with the back of her forefinger.

'Julia. . .!' Nick ground out through gritted teeth and she took pity on him, giving his balls one last, friendly squeeze before turning her attention back to his cock. As she began to stroke it lightly, Nick seemed to lose patience. He sat up and crushed her to him, kissing her with a ferocity which took her by surprise.

'Don't play games with me, Julia,' he whispered as they broke apart.

'Games? I – o-ooh!'

She tangled her hands in his hair and held his forehead against hers as he suddenly lifted her by the hips and brought her down on his upright cock. The penetration was so deep that Julia felt herself grow hot again, her throat grew dry and she felt an ache high up, at the neck of her womb.

Once again Nick had taken charge, she acknowledged fleetingly, and once again she had allowed him to do so. She would have to rationalise it all later, right now her body was sending unmistakable, urgent messages to her brain which she could not ignore.

Their foreheads came together again and Julia stared deep into Nick's now dark grey eyes. At that moment there was nothing else in the world for her, no other reality except Nick and the melding of their two bodies. She could feel his heart pumping steadily in his chest, and the shallow, ragged cadence of his breathing as he struggled to control himself. The smiling, teasing boy was gone now, in his place a strongly aroused man who was driven to achieving the ultimate release.

His hands were still gripping her by the hips and he lifted her now, supporting her weight so that her knees resting on the bed either side of him served merely as balance. Vaguely, Julia was aware of the contraction of his biceps, the straining of the tendons in his neck as he moved his head back, away from hers.

Her conscious attention, though, was focused

on the silky, cleated walls of her vagina as they clutched instinctively at the warm, hard shaft which was now poised at the entrance to her body. She cried out as Nick finally allowed her to sink back down on to his lap and she was filled again, the dark channel expanding to accommodate the full width of him.

His mouth was set into a grim line of concentration as he lifted her again and Julia pressed her lips against his bottom lip, nipping at it with her teeth. His breath came out on a sigh as she sank back down again.

Looking at his intent, set face, Julia was suddenly overcome by the urge to make him lose that incredible control. His eyes were already glazed so that she felt he was removed from her. She determined to bring him back. Linking her hands behind his neck, under his hair, Julia concentrated on contracting and releasing her intimate muscles in time with Nick's carefully controlled strokes.

He looked directly at her and his lips curved upwards slightly, as if acknowledging that battle had been enjoined. With each downward stroke, Julia's bottom was squashed against the hardness of his thighs. As he plunged into her to the hilt, she deliberately allowed her muscles to relax, so that her buttocks splayed softly over his legs and his balls bounced lightly against the exposed, stretched membranes of her sex.

The first time this happened, Nick gasped slightly and Julia felt him twitch inside her. Realising she had found the key, the next time he brought her down, she squirmed slightly on his lap, stimulating the over-sensitised skin of his scrotum.

Moving her hands up to cup his head, she held him firmly in front of her so that she could watch his face. Nick frowned, his lips parted and his eyes narrowed. He lifted her up one more time, this time pushing her down hard on to his lap, impaling her.

Julia cried out as the tip of his penis battered against the entrance to her womb and the vibration reverberated through her lower belly. Then the first hot spurt of semen flooded her and Nick pressed her sweat-slick body against his as he gave in to the inevitable. Still holding his face between her hands, Julia watched the expressions dance across his face; a glorious mix of defeat and triumph, of relief and ecstasy.

Squeezing him tightly from within, she pressed her open mouth against his so that their breath mingled and their hearts beat as one.

At last he was still and they rolled with exquisitely choreographed precision on to the pillows. Nick made no attempt to withdraw his spent penis from her, and Julia was glad to hold him close for a little while longer. They did not speak, though Julia sensed that he was as awed by the intensity of what had happened between them as she.

Pulling the sheets up to cover their rapidly cooling bodies, Julia snuggled contentedly in his arms. Nick caressed her back with long, rhythmic strokes and it wasn't long before she felt sleep steal over her.

*

Julia woke the next morning to find herself alone. She stretched, relishing the warmth of the bright spring sunshine pouring through the uncurtained window and playing across her naked skin. Nick had woken her in the middle of the night and made love to her again, with more leisureliness this time, and once again they had fallen asleep curled tightly together, spoon-fashion.

Sniffing, Julia realised that there was bacon cooking in the kitchen. Wrapping the sheet around her, she trailed it through the flat to the kitchen door. Nick was frying bacon in a pan, stark-naked, completely oblivious to the danger of the spitting fat.

'You're awake at last, then?' he said, turning to smile at her. 'Bacon butties for breakfast – I don't know about you, but I'm starving!'

Julia smiled.

'I'll go and get some clothes on.'

'Oh no you don't!' He stopped her by grabbing her by the arm and manoeuvring her into one of the kitchen chairs. 'This is ready to eat and, besides, you look lovely just as you are.'

Julia smiled weakly. She wasn't so confident about displaying her thirty-seven-year-old body in broad daylight, but she could hardly tell him that without bringing his attention to its failings! Besides, he was walking around her kitchen quite unselfconsciously naked, apparently oblivious to Julia's surreptitious interest in his penis swinging gently between his legs.

She had never thought of a man's penis as being a thing of beauty before, particularly not in its unaroused state. Yet there was something quite attractive about Nick's, something almost innocent. . .

'Julia?'

She looked up in surprise as he broke into her thoughts. Taking the plate he was offering her, she smiled somewhat sheepishly before tucking in. She wondered, briefly, what she should say now. It had never occurred to her before that there might be a 'morning-after' etiquette, and now that she was in that situation, she wasn't quite sure how to proceed.

Having spent the night, would Nick expect to spend the day with her? Would he now consider them to be a 'couple'? Was that what she wanted?

Thankfully, she was saved from embarrassing herself by Nick breaking into her thoughts.

'I have to be off in a few minutes – my parents are expecting me for Sunday lunch.'

'Oh – right.'

Now that he had taken the initiative and was leaving, Julia felt unaccountably miffed. Exasperated with herself, she smiled at him.

'Leave the clearing up – I'll do it later.'

He nodded and disappeared into the bathroom. Julia heard the shower running as she poured herself a second cup of tea from the pot. When he came out a little later, he was fully dressed, his wet hair slicked back off his face and secured with an elastic tie. Regarding him lazily, Julia realised anew what a very attractive man he was.

'You won't forget you're going to be calling into the college this week to check out the course, will you?'

Julia shook her head.

'I won't forget.'

'Right. The course director's name is Pete Finch. Oh yeah – apparently he's a bit of an octopus, so I should watch out for him behind the cookers if I were you!'

He bent down to kiss her cheek. Just as she thought he was going to straighten and leave without another word, he said, his voice low, 'Will you come round to my place later in the week? I'll cook you something . . . sustaining.'

Julia's lips curved into a soft smile. She shivered as his breath caressed her neck and played across the tips of her partially exposed breasts.

'Why not?' she whispered.

Crooking his forefinger under her chin, he tilted her head so that he could find her lips with his. The kiss was so sweet, so tender, Julia was filled with such a yearning that she felt unexpected tears prick her eyelids.

'I'll call you.'

Then he was gone, leaving her to contemplate the dirty dishes.

Greg watched from behind the curtains of his bedroom as Nick ran down the steps of the house and unlocked the door to his battered old van. He drew back slightly as he turned and glanced back up towards the windows at the top of the house.

Even from where he was standing Greg could see the contented smile playing around the other man's mouth and he swallowed, hard. He had watched them go up the stairs together the night before and he had been shocked by the surge of jealousy he had felt. At first he had been surprised at how young Julia's boyfriend had been, but then, he told himself, she was an attractive woman, any man would find her appealing, regardless of age. He trembled slightly as he imagined what an experienced *older* woman like Julia could teach him. . .

He thought of Kerry who worked with him on Saturdays at the burger bar. Kerry was small and red-haired and Greg had been in love with her for months. Kerry was always nice to him, but he hadn't ever dared to ask her out, let alone try to form a relationship with her. How could he when the sum total of his sexual experience was an inconvenient erection every time his maths teacher leaned over his shoulder to check his work?

It was something about the light, floral perfume she wore, coupled with the closeness of her large, soft breasts . . . he would only have to turn his face and his cheek would brush against them. . .

Come to think of it, Mrs Matthews looked a lot like Julia. She had the same air of self-assurance and a firm, full figure which hinted at hidden delights . . . Greg jumped as he heard the door to the flat upstairs open and close and Julia's light footsteps pass his doorway on the way downstairs.

Greg sighed. She might be gorgeous and she might like younger men, but he had no illusions about himself. He was nothing like as good-looking as the guy who had just driven away and he had no experience whatsoever. Why would she ever look twice at *him*? It was a pleasant fantasy, nothing more.

Turning on his Anglepoise lamp, he switched on his computer and prepared to immerse himself in the complicated new program he was working on, pushing away the discomforting thought that he would far rather be immersing himself in Julia's delectable body instead.

Downstairs, Julia tapped lightly on the door of her landlady's studio, waiting until she heard a cheerful 'come in' before turning the old-fashioned door handle. Fenella Learman treated her to a huge, welcoming smile as she looked up from her easel.

'Ah Julia! Good-morning. Would you like to join me for some coffee?'

'Morning, Mrs Learman. Coffee would be lovely, thanks.'

'Please call me Fenella – I don't like things to be too formal, do you? Have a seat. It's lovely and sunny in the window.' Wiping her hands on an old towel, she disappeared through a side door, leaving Julia to make herself comfortable on the window seat. She was right; it *was* warm with the mid-morning sunshine streaming through the glass. She could see the garden outside, a riot of colour and greenery which, on first glance, looked overgrown but was, as she could see when she looked more closely, a well-planned and executed 'wild garden'.

Fenella reappeared minutes later bearing a tray laden with a huge coffee pot and two chunky earthenware mugs.

'Sugar and milk?'

'Just milk, please. I was just admiring your garden – do you look after it yourself?'

Fenella's broad, friendly face softened as she followed Julia's gaze.

'Oh absolutely! I can't think of many better ways of spending a Sunday afternoon. You're welcome to give me a hand whenever you're free.'

Julia smiled, warmed by the genuine good intention in the other woman's offer.

'That would be lovely, thank you.'

She regarded Fenella more closely as she sipped her coffee. She was probably in her early fifties, though her hair was growing prematurely grey. Fenella wore it scraped back in an uncompromising bun. On most women the old-fashioned style would be ageing, but it seemed just right on Fenella, the wispy tendrils framing her broad, unlined face with its small, almost *retrousée* nose and generous mouth. She was what most people would kindly call 'pleasantly plump' and she had the most beautiful violet-coloured eyes Julia had ever seen.

Those eyes were scrutinising Julia now in much the same way as she was looking at her and Julia smiled.

'I meant to ask you if it was all right to have overnight guests? I hadn't meant to be rude last night. . .'

Fenella laughed, a gusty, echoing guffaw which took Julia by surprise.

'Mind? Of course I don't mind! I must admit, my own taste runs to a slightly more mature vintage, but each to his own.'

104

The last was said with such a wicked twinkle in her eye that Julia burst out laughing. She had instinctively liked Fenella from the first moment she met her and she felt sure that they could easily become friends. As if reading her mind, Fenella said suddenly, 'I think you and I will get along just fine, Julia. The thing with younger men, of course, is that they tend to be so much more . . . shall we say *malleable* than their fathers. At least, that is, once one gets past that annoying laddishness that so many of them seem to display these days.'

Remembering how exciting she had found Paul's capitulation, Julia sat forward, her chin in her palm.

'I'm intrigued! You sound as if you're speaking from experience,' she said.

'You'd be surprised! I think there are probably a lot of men whose first sexual encounter was with a sympathetic older woman.'

'Do you really think that's the appeal for them? The thought that they'll get a sympathetic response?' She wasn't sure why, but Julia felt vaguely dismayed by the idea.

Fenella chuckled at her expression.

'I think that's a part, though by no means all of the story. Why don't you ask your young man?'

'He's not *my* young man, Fenella.'

'Ah, I see – like to play the field, do you?'

Julia shrugged.

'I might. To be honest with you, I haven't really had the time to find out yet!'

Fenella regarded her thoughtfully for a few moments.

'You know, Julia, if you enjoy the particular charms of very young men, there could well be something you could help me with. . .' She trailed off and Julia looked at her expectantly.

'Go on – I'm intrigued!' she prompted, but Fenella merely smiled at her, rather enigmatically, Julia felt.

'No, that's for later. As for now . . . have you met my son, Greg?'

'Yes – you sent him up to check I was all right yesterday, remember?'

'Of course. Do you have children?'

'Two, a boy and a girl, both slightly older than Greg.'

'They're a worry, aren't they?'

Julia waited patiently while Fenella stared out of the window, sure that she would continue when she was ready. She was not disappointed.

'Greg is such a solitary boy, always closeted away up there with his computer. It's not right – a boy of that age should be out in the world, preferably sowing a few wild oats into the bargain.'

Julia laughed.

'I'm sure he will, when he's ready.'

Fenella looked at her slightly strangely.

'You're probably right,' she said at last. 'Of course, in years gone by, if Greg had a father he would probably have taken him to an obliging older woman who would have taught him what was what. Anyway – would you like to see some of my paintings?'

Julia was taken aback by the abrupt change of subject. For a moment there she was convinced that Fenella's words held some purpose, even that she was suggesting . . . but no, that would be absurd! Surely no mother would suggest that her lodger should relieve her son of his virginity?

Scanning Fenella's features, Julia realised that she was giving nothing away.

'This is Darren,' she was saying, turning a large canvas to face her. 'What do you think?'

Julia's eyebrows shot up towards her hairline. 'Darren' was a portrait of a young, nude male. He was standing, his chin tipped downward and a heavy frown between his dark eyes which were glowering beneath his lowered brows. His arms were folded across his chest, his hips thrust out with palpable defiance, almost as if he was posing against his will. His penis was long, and lovingly described by the painter, very pale against the coarse dark hair surrounding it.

'It's very . . . impressive,' Julia replied faintly.

Fenella chuckled, leaning the portrait against the wall.

'I thought he might be to your taste – he is a very virile-looking young man, isn't he?'

'Yes . . . do you often paint nudes?'

'Sometimes. I like the human form in all its different shapes and sizes, but I have to admit, it was a treat to work on a perfect specimen like young Darren here. . .' She looked up as the door opened and Greg put his head round. 'Hello, love – come in and join us.'

Julia noticed that Greg's eyes skittered in her direction without actually catching her gaze and she smiled encouragingly.

'I was just admiring your mother's work,' she

told him, noticing from the corner of her eye that Fenella had unobtrusively turned 'Darren' so that he was facing the wall.

'She's good, isn't she?' Mother and son smiled fondly at each other and Julia realised that Greg's awkwardness was probably only reserved for other women.

She studied him surreptitiously as he sat down, noticing the long, lean length of his legs and the way his dark hair flopped forward as he bent down to pick up a sketch. If only he wasn't so awkward, holding himself as if he hoped no one would notice him, he would really be quite an attractive young man.

'Did you see Kerry yesterday at work?' Fenella asked him and Julia was intrigued to see a dark stain of colour seep up over his cheekbones.

'Of course.'

'Why don't you take the bull by the horns and ask her out?' Fenella asked as she poured him a drink in the mug she herself used. 'After all, the worst thing that could happen is that she could say no.'

'*Mother*!' Greg said in an aggrieved undertone, tilting his head in Julia's direction.

Fenella grimaced.

'Sorry.'

'I'll take this upstairs, if you don't mind – I only wanted a quick break from the computer screen. See you later.'

Fenella watched him go, a frown scoring a line between her eyes.

'I seem to have developed a knack for putting my foot in it where that young man is concerned!'

108

she said ruefully when the door had closed behind him. 'Sorry you had to hear that, Julia.'

'Don't worry – I've been through it myself.' Julia dismissed Fenella's concern with a wave of her hand. 'After all, isn't it a mother's place to be in the wrong? I'd best be getting back upstairs so you can get on.'

'Before you go – I shall be going away over next weekend. I wonder . . . would you . . . look after Greg for me?'

Julia was about to retort that, while she would be more than happy to keep a maternal eye on Greg, she was sure he wouldn't appreciate the idea of a babysitter, when she realised that Fenella had put a definite inflection on the phrase *look after*. For a moment she held Fenella's eye as she thought about the shy young man who so far hadn't managed to look directly at her for more than a few seconds at a time, and she smiled slowly.

'I'll see what I can do,' she said softly.

Fenella gave her a searching look, then she smiled, quite serenely.

'He's a good boy, really – he shouldn't give you much trouble,' she said calmly and once again Julia felt confused.

Leaving Fenlla bending happily over her work, she walked slowly up the stairs. On the second landing, there was a full-length mirror bolted to the wall and she paused, staring at her reflection thoughtfully for a few moments. Suddenly, she had the overwhelming feeling that someone was watching her and she turned her head to her left.

She had been so wrapped up in her thoughts

that she hadn't realised she had paused outside Greg's bedroom and that the door was half-open. The room was in darkness apart from the yellow-toned spotlight illuminating the desk. Greg was sitting in front of his computer, his face ghostly pale in the reflected grey light from the screen.

He seemed mesmerised by the sight of her standing in front of the mirror and, for an instant as their eyes met, Julia saw the swift flare of desire in his. Then it was gone and he was mumbling an apology for staring at her.

'It's all right, Greg,' she said gently. 'It was I who stopped right outside your bedroom door. I'll leave you to your work now.' Smiling to herself, she went upstairs to the flat.

Chapter Seven

JULIA STOOD OUTSIDE the college late on Thursday afternoon and gazed up at its vast, glass-fronted façade. By the time she'd finished at the coffee shop and dashed back to the flat to tidy herself up, she had been half-inclined to put the visit off still longer. Only the thought of Nick and Gavin's combined nagging had pushed her out again.

Now here she was, standing outside with the prospectus clutched in her hand, wondering what she was doing here. Before, trapped in a dull marriage and a job with few prospects, the idea of going to college had seemed like an exciting option. Now, though, there were so many other things in her life to excite her, she wasn't so sure that this was what she wanted after all.

Still, she was here now – she might as well take a look around. Pete Finch, the course director, came down to meet her. He was a short, spindly little man, prematurely balding. His eyes were the only really attractive feature in an otherwise forgettable face – they were large, limpid and a deep, velvety brown. Eyes to drown in, if one could ignore the rest of him. The moment he opened his mouth Julia wondered how one so inherently soulless could possibly possess such expressive eyes.

'Julia, isn't it?' Nick told me you'd be coming in to look around. We have quite a few, shall we say, more *mature* students on our catering course this year. The interest for our older girls comes from years in the kitchen, I suppose, eh?' He chortled at what he clearly thought was a witticism of the first order and Julia forced a tight little smile. 'This way, this way. We've still one or two places left for this academic year – you've not missed too much.'

He pressed his hand unnecessarily against the small of her back and urged her along the corridor. Even through her linen blouse Julia could feel that the skin of his palm was hot and clammy and she moved away pointedly.

'Most of the students have left to go home by now, I'm afraid,' he told her when they found the first of the kitchens deserted.

The fresh, pungent scent of lemons and warm sponge cake lingered in the air and Julia sniffed appreciatively.

'Lemon pudding,' Finch supplied helpfully.

As he spoke, his hot, slightly stale breath touched her cheek and Julia realised he was standing awfully close. Trying to move along the row of cookers discreetly, she searched her mind for a whole barrage of questions with which she could distract him. It had been a long time since Julia had met anyone quite as obnoxious as Peter Finch and she was heartily relieved when the secretary poked her head around the door to tell him that he was wanted on the telephone.

Clearly annoyed at being interrupted, he muttered something to Julia about taking a look round herself and to bring any further queries to the reception desk, before he scurried self-importantly out of the door.

Once she was alone in the room, Julia took more interest in it. Even without the irritation of being harassed by the director, though, she knew she couldn't really see herself relearning the cooking methods she had developed over the years. She'd just have a quick look at the machinery, then she'd go.

It was as she was bending over a table to read a discarded menu plan that she sensed someone come into the room behind her. Before she had time to straighten and turn, strong hands clamped round her eyes and a firm body pinned her to the table.

'Don't move,' a deep voice whispered in her ear.

For a split second, Julia thought Finch had come back in, and she panicked. But the hands moving round to caress her breasts were familiar and the soft brush of hair against her cheek made her smile.

'Nick!' she whispered, moving her head so that she could kiss him.

'Don't move,' he whispered.

She could hear the smile in his voice as clearly

113

as she could feel the hardness of his erection pressing urgently into the soft flesh of her left buttock. She gasped at his fingers curled around the hem of her skirt and began to ease it upward.

'Nick! We can't. . .! Someone might come!'

'Let them – I want you.'

Julia closed her eyes as his lips trailed a burning path from her ear down the side of her neck to her collarbone. Having hitched her skirt up around her waist, he made short work of her briefs, dragging them down to mid-thigh before unfastening his own clothing and releasing his erection.

His lips curved against her neck as his fingers encountered the hot, welling centre of her. It was all the confirmation that he needed that she wanted him too. She had become so ready for him in that short space of time that her body welcomed the swift stab of his penis without the slightest protest. Julia gasped as he began to move inside her, all the while muttering sweet obscenities in her ear. His breath was hot and fragrant, the feel of it sending delicious shivers right through her as it caressed her skin.

Julia felt herself grow warm as Nick's fingers played expertly on the small scrap of flesh which was pushed out by the pressure of his sex enmeshed with hers. Oblivious to the cold metal of the table pressing into her belly, she thrust her vulva shamelessly against his fingertips, rotating her hips against his thrusting body like a cat on heat.

Somehow the idea that someone could walk in at any moment and discover them, coupled with the sheer unexpectedness of Nick's arrival added an extra edge to Julia's pleasure and she came, swiftly, minutes before Nick.

Only as she began to emerge from the mists of satisfaction did she realise that there were footsteps in the corridor, coming steadily closer. Panicking, she moved away from Nick and adjusted her skirt, while he moved discreetly behind a filing cabinet to button his fly. Only just in time, for the door opened and Peter Finch bustled in.

'Ah, Julia – how are we getting on? Have you decided to join our happy little crew? Oh – Nick – I didn't see you there when I came in!'

The man's disappointment at seeing Nick was so obvious that Julia was hard-pressed not to laugh. How he could fail to notice her dishevelled state, or the tension in the room, was testament to the man's complete self-absorption. Nick winked at Julia and she glared at him for daring to try to make her laugh.

'Thank you, Mr Finch,' she said, conscious of the quaver in her voice even if he wasn't, 'I think I've seen enough now. Nick has been able to answer *all* my questions.'

'Oh. Well, I hope we might see you again before too long.'

He followed Julia and Nick along the corridor. Julia didn't dare look at Nick until the director was safely out of the way. Then they both collapsed into fits of laughter.

'Really, Nick,' she said when she had recovered herself, 'what if he'd come in five minutes before?'

'You're even more beautiful when you laugh,' he replied irrelevantly. 'I have to go. Can you come to dinner on Saturday?'

'Oh, no, not this weekend. I promised to do my landlady a favour.' Julia thought of shy young Greg and smiled inwardly.

If Nick was put out that she wasn't free he didn't show it.

'Next Wednesday, then? Ah, no, I've got a disco then. How about Thursday?'

Julia nodded. Seeing him less than once a week could hardly be called a hot affair, could it? Plenty of time for her to try out her wings in between their highly satisfactory encounters.

'I'll see you then,' she murmured, leaning forward to kiss him briefly on the cheek.

She could feel him watching her as she walked away from him along the corridor. At the end, she turned and waggled the fingers of one hand at him. He waved back and Julia left the building feeling warm inside. He really was the most *likeable* man, quite apart from anything else!

The rest of the week passed slowly. Julia followed her impulse to continue her current pattern of change and went to the hairdressers. Once there, she swapped her long, straight brown bob for a wavy, short style with auburn lowlights. She felt pounds lighter without the heavy tresses hanging on her shoulders and she consciously held her head up as she walked down the street, refusing to miss the feel of it around her face.

Michael hated it.

'What have you done to yourself?' were his first

116

words to her as she walked through the door of the house.

'Hello Michael – you're looking well too,' she replied drily, casting her eyes around the familiar living-room. In less than two weeks Michael had reduced it to a sty. Dirty dishes were piled up on the floor at the end of the sofa and a week's worth of newspapers had been discarded, willy-nilly, on the coffee table. It depressed her, this evidence of how she had, until now, spent her time – clearing up after other people.

'Why am I here, Michael?' she asked him when he didn't speak. 'Not because you've run out of cups and expect me to wash some up for you, I trust?'

'Bitch,' Michael said good-naturedly.

Julia perched on the arm of the sofa.

'I must admit, I hadn't expected you to be living here still.'

'I told you things were over between me and Gail.'

'Being difficult is she? Don't worry, Michael – she'll come round, eventually. After all, she's waited for you for a long time, hasn't she?'

Michael avoided her eye and she guessed that she had hit on the truth. He was trying to persuade Gail to restart their relationship now that Julia had left him. If she had any lingering doubts, his next words confirmed it.

'I thought we should discuss what we're going to do about the house. It's far too big for one. I thought I'd rent something smaller, nearer to school.'

Even though she was confident that the

decision she had made to leave him was the right one, and that it was totally irreversible, Julia hesitated momentarily before making the final step.

'This time of year is a good time to sell,' she said at last.

Michael held her eye steadily.

'You're sure that's what you want?'

She nodded.

'Yes.'

'Very well. I'll contact the agents in the morning. You realise, of course, that after the mortgage is paid you'll only be entitled to about ten thousand pounds?'

'We'll see. Well, if that's settled, I'd better get back to work.'

'Julia?' Michael's voice stopped her at the door and she turned, regarding him quizzically. 'We'll keep in touch, won't we?'

Julia felt herself soften towards him.

'Michael – we've been together half my lifetime. Of course we'll keep in touch. We've still got two children, remember?'

He nodded and, for a moment, she caught a glimpse of the young man with whom she had fallen in love all those years ago. He looked almost diffident, standing in the doorway between the hall and the living-room, his hands thrust deep into his trouser pockets. Her hand dropped from the door handle and she walked slowly back towards him.

'Michael . . . it'll all turn out for the best, you'll see.'

He didn't answer, he simply put his hands on

118

her shoulders and pulled her towards him. Julia considered moving away, but his touch was so familiar, she felt a little of the old attraction creep beneath her defences.

His lips were warm and firm with a faint taste of fine malt whisky. As he kissed her, he closed his eyes and brought his hands up to cradle her head. Julia parted her lips and let his tongue probe urgently at the softness inside her mouth, surprised by how quickly she caught fire. Her body knew him so well, it seemed it was still conditioned to respond to the old, familiar stimulus regardless of how her mind told it they were no longer a couple.

Briefly, as she felt his hands pull her blouse out of the waistband of her trousers, she wondered why he could never be this spontaneous before. It crossed her mind that it might not be altogether wise to make love with her estranged husband in the middle of the afternoon, but then she thought – what the hell? They *were* still married, technically at least and it would be pleasant to get on well together for a change.

She sensed the need in him, the very real desire to prove himself in some way. Her leaving him must have knocked his confidence, for she realised that he had never really expected that she would go through with it. Would he have behaved differently throughout their marriage if she had been more assertive before?

Michael's large, cool hands brushed the tender skin of her belly and Julia gasped, eschewing all rational thought for later. Now she wanted only to touch him as he was touching her, to try to relive some of the rapture they had once known together.

'Julia. . .' His breath was hot in her ear and she felt him tremble.

Taking pity on him she helped him to undo her buttons, riffling her fingers through his hair as he immediately dipped his head to nuzzle the deep valley between her breasts. The lacy cups of her 'uplift' bra strained as her breasts swelled in response, peaking into two button-hard crests which rubbed against the delicate material.

By now Julia had managed to open Michael's shirt and she urged him upright so that she could press herself against the warm, naked skin of his chest. His fingers dispensed with the fastening to her bra with practised ease and it dropped on to the floor at their feet. Michael lifted both her breasts and kissed them lingeringly, each in turn, as if greeting long-lost friends.

'Julia, Julia, I—'

'Ssh!' she placed the tips of her fingers against his lips to silence him. Smiling as he frowned, she shook her head. 'No words, Michael. Let's just love. . .'

He caught her fingertips between his teeth and nipped gently at them while with his hands he unfastened first her trousers, then his own. Julia backed him up until they reached the high-backed armchair by the fire and he sank slowly down on to it. Looking up at her through heated eyes, he watched as she eased her trousers over her hips and stepped out of them. Her briefs followed and she stood quietly looking down at him, enjoying the way his eyes roved longingly over the naked body which must, after all, be so familiar to him.

From the look on his face, though, one would have thought that he had forgotten every line and curve. His hands came up almost reverently to stroke the sensitive undersides of her breasts as she bent over to kiss him.

Slowly, she sank to her knees and, with a glance at his tense face, she pulled his trousers and briefs down, over his hips and along the length of his legs. His cock sprang free, pointing straight up from his belly. Julia hid a smile as she saw her name emblazoned along its length. The ink had faded, of course, but not nearly as much as she would have expected. She wondered how he had tried to explain away the bizarre tattoo to Gail – if he'd got this far in his campaign to win her back.

Dropping a mischievous kiss on its end, Julia turned slowly, presenting Michael with a prime view of her rounded bottom. Looking at him over her shoulder, she parted her legs and backed up so that she was sitting on his lap, settling herself so that she could feel the slender length of his aroused penis pointing up her back.

Michael was breathing shallowly now and his hands, as he brought them round to cup her full breasts, were trembling. Julia closed her eyes for a few moments as he squeezed and kneaded the voluptuous flesh, wriggling her hips slightly at the same time so that the lips of her sex opened to kiss the hairy surface of his scrotum. She felt his cock twitch against her spine in response and knew that the time had come to take things a step further.

Leaning forward, Julia placed her hands on his

knees to brace herself while she slowly lifted her bottom. Michael made a small, incoherent sound in the back of his throat as he was presented with a view of her rear end in all its glory. Julia imagined what he could see: her round white bottom, split like a peach down the middle to reveal the darker flesh of the crease and the tight, puckered opening to her body which she normally kept hidden. And below, the soft, moist purse of her sex would be fully exposed, like a ripe, juicy fruit just waiting to be sampled.

Slowly, so slowly she could feel the tremble of Michael's breath in the still air, Julia reached behind herself and sank her fingers in the pulpy flesh, pulling her sex-lips apart so that the entrance to her body was stretched, ready to enclose him. Replying with alacrity to the blatant invitation, Michael guided the head of his penis so that it rested against her opening and Julia moved her hips slightly so that it slipped inside, no more than half an inch.

Teasingly, she held him there for a full minute before, with exquisite slowness, she sank back down on to his lap, drawing the long, hard length of his penis inside her.

The breath hissed between Michael's clenched teeth as her silky sheath folded round him and he laid his cheek against her back. Julia shivered as she felt him kiss the sensitive skin between her shoulder blades and she reached up, behind her head, to grasp his neck as he sat upright and pulled her close against him.

'Oh Julia. . .'

She moved herself up and down with

increasing urgency as his hot breath fanned her cheek and his hands clutched rhythmically against her stretched breasts. Sliding her forefinger down the front of her own body, she found the stiff, hard button of her clitoris and began to rub it gently, bathing it in the clear, sticky fluid seeping from her own body.

Looking across the room, she could see them reflected dimly in the shiny marble of the fireplace. She looked sleek, impossibly wanton as she writhed on Michael's lap, her naked form stretched upward, her breasts thrust out.

Her climax crept up on her, a gradual, spreading warmth which radiated out from the core of her, running through her torso and along her limbs. And as her inner lips began to pulse and throb, they triggered Michael's orgasm so that he came at the same time, flooding her passage with hot, milky fluid which seeped out again, bathing his thrusting penis in its own emissions.

When, at last, the sensations began to fade, Julia climbed off his lap and turned to face him as she dressed. He was looking at her with a sense of wonder, oblivious to the sticky pool of their combined fluids drying rapidly on his thighs as he watched Julia tidy herself. He made no attempt to move as she picked up her bag and slipped her arms into the sleeves of her jacket.

'You're going?' he said at last, as if he couldn't quite believe the evidence of his own eyes.

Julia looked at him, saw the yearning in his eyes which he couldn't, or did not care to conceal and she felt her heart constrict in her chest. It would be so easy to stay, to agree to try again. For one interminable second, Julia leaned towards the safer solution. Michael recognised the struggle in her and his eyes lit up, anticipating her capitulation.

She half took a step towards him, than an image of Nick's calm grey eyes popped, unbidden, into her mind and pulled her back to her senses. She didn't want to give him up, not just yet.

The realisation surprised her slightly and she raised her eyebrows, tearing her eyes away from Michael's as she did so. She hadn't bargained on Nick becoming important to her. It wasn't just Nick though, she acknowledged silently. If she came back now it might be all right for a month or two, but then they would quickly slip into their old habit of taking each other for granted.

'I must go,' she replied, at last. 'Let me know how you get on at the estate agents. Take care, Michael.'

Blowing him a kiss, she left, feeling much happier than she had when she'd first arrived.

'Yoo-hoo! Julia!'

She turned as she heard Louise's unmistakable greeting from the house next door.

'Louise! How are you?'

'So-so. Got time for a coffee?'

Julia glanced discreetly at her watch, then shrugged. What was the point of hurrying home to cook tea for just herself?

'I should think so.'

Glancing swiftly at the house she had just left, she hurried up Louise's pathway, hoping that

124

Michael hadn't seen that she hadn't gone straight home. She didn't want to prolong their good-byes after what had just happened between them.

'So – how's it going?' Louise said as soon as the coffee was made.

Julia settled herself comfortably in her ex-neighbour's lemon and blue chintz armchair and smiled enigmatically.

'How's what going?' she asked innocently, grinning at Louise's frustrated expression.

'You know damn well what I mean, Julia Penn – how's your sex-life?'

'Very well, thank you,' Julia teased. 'How's yours?'

'Oh, since you left Ken and I have been at it like rabbits, just like all the other long-married couples we know, I suspect.

'Excuse me?'

'Well, all the guys start to feel insecure if it happens to someone like you and Michael, don't they? I mean, they start to think, "If old Michael's wife could do it, so could mine, couldn't she?" You've done the rest of us a favour, gal – spiced things up a bit!'

Julia wasn't sure whether to be amused or insulted.

'So I'm the subversive in the street now, am I?'

'Absolutely! If Ken knew you were in here talking to me now he'd have forty fits!'

'But we've had coffee together at least once a week for the past twelve years!'

'That was different.'

'Different? How?'

'Then you were a dutiful little wife, just like me.

Now you might infect me with your mid-life crisis and encourage me to run off on my own!' Louise laughed her light, tinkling laugh, but Julia felt more dismayed than amused.

'Is that what everyone's saying – that I'm having a mid-life crisis? How depressing!'

'Isn't it? I suppose that's what the blokes are saying, down the pub. It probably makes Michael feel better – makes your leaving him less personal, if you know what I mean!'

Julia stared morosely into her coffee mug.

'It's just not fair, Louise!' she blurted suddenly. Louise looked startled and Julia tried to smooth out the fierce scowl which she knew was puckering her forehead. 'Well – I mean to say – no one batted an eyelid when Michael was having an affair, did they? I suppose all the "good old boys" at the pub thought that was a great wheeze. *Good old Michael, he's a lad, isn't he, eh?* Why is it so different for me? Why do they have to assume that I'm menopausal just because I want some fun in my life?'

Louise looked genuinely perplexed by Julia's outburst and she patted her hand awkwardly.

'Well, it's not as if you've left Michael for someone else, is it? I mean . . . you're not having an affair, as such, are you?'

'Would that make it more acceptable?' Julia felt quite shocked. 'Honestly, Louise – I want my independence, that doesn't make me round the twist! Besides,' she smiled conspiratorially, her anger evaporating as quickly as it had come, 'I'm having rather a good time. *That's* what all the old gossips can't stand!'

Louise, clearly relieved that Julia had climbed down off her high horse, leaned forward expectantly.

'Come on, Julia – give!'

'Oh, I am doing . . . and taking, actually, in equal measure! I don't know, Louise, for a moment when I was with Michael earlier, I seriously wondered whether I was doing the right thing. But, the thing is, I feel so . . . so much younger on my own. I'm just not ready to settle down with my knitting and a hot-water bottle yet, I want to kick up my heels while I'm still young enough. Anyway, I'd better get off.'

She laughed at Louise's exasperated exclamation.

'But you haven't told me anything!'

'Come and see me in my new flat one evening – we'll have a good old gossip then.'

She wrote down the address on the back of an old envelope before handing it back to Louise.

'You do know that I'm your friend, Julia, don't you?' Louise said suddenly as the two women reached the door.

Julia turned towards her in surprise.

'Of course. I'm not thinking that you'd gossip about me, Lou, if that's what you're worrying about. It's just that I haven't got everything sorted out in my own mind yet. You will come and see me, won't you?'

Louise hugged her.

'Of course I will. And Julia?' Julia paused, her hand on the doorknob, looking back at Louise expectantly. Louise smiled, almost shyly at her. 'Just for the record – I think you're very brave.'

'*Brave?*'

'Yes. It takes guts to choose to be on your own after all these years. I hope you are having a good time, I really do.'

Julia leaned forward and kissed her friend gently on the cheek. Her skin was velvet-soft and smelled faintly of face powder.

'Thanks, Louise,' she said softly, then she opened the door and slipped outside, eager, suddenly, to get back to her own little flat.

Chapter Eight

THAT FRIDAY FENELLA left for her weekend away with a hug for Greg and a meaningful glance at Julia. Greg seemed completely oblivious to his mother's machinations and he was unable to hide his surprise when Julia offered to cook him supper that evening.

'That's if you're not planning to go out, of course,' she added hastily.

'No, I . . . thanks. I'll come up later than, shall I?'

Julia smiled.

'About eight would be good. Maybe we can get to know each other a little better, since we're going to be living at such close quarters.'

Greg shot her a startled glance and for a moment Julia thought she'd gone too far and frightened him off. Gently does it, she reminded herself. She didn't want to put him off women for the rest of his life!

Greg retreated to his room to think things over.

What had Julia meant by that last remark? He began to tremble as he imagined the unimaginable. He'd read about older women, even knew one boy at school who had been initiated into the mysterious arts of love by his next door neighbour, if he was to be believed.

Deciding he'd better take a bath, just in case, he laid out some clean clothes on the bed and made for the bathroom. The small, square room quickly filled with steam and he undressed slowly, thinking about Julia.

He liked her new hairstyle – the short, shiny cut clung fetchingly to her skull, leaving her well-sculpted features exposed. He had stared at her, when he was sure she wasn't aware that he was looking, so that he could recall the precise details of her face and figure just by closing his eyes.

Climbing into the hot water, he lay back, letting the small waves wash over him, easing the sudden tension which had invaded his limbs. Closing his eyes he thought of Julia. Her direct hazel eyes always seemed to hold a smile, as if she was laughing at some small, private joke, though not in a mocking way; she had never made him feel small. Not like some of the girls his own age who seemed so knowing. He sensed, though, that Julia had somehow guessed how he felt about her, but that she didn't mind.

Not only did she not mind, but there was something about the way she had looked at him earlier which made him think there was more to her invitation to supper then the offer of a simple meal. Something . . . *assessing* in her glance.

Surely she couldn't fancy *him*? Opening his eyes, Greg stared down at his skinny body now submerged in the water and grimaced. His skin was so white, since he never liked to bare it to the sun when there were other people around. Now it had been turned a deep, unattractive pink by the hot water, his small purple nipples, drawn into two small, turgid peaks which broke the surface.

He was certainly no oil painting, but there was nothing overtly off-putting about his body, as far as he could tell. Certainly, down *there* he was all man. He was rather proud of his penis – it was long and thin, very straight, with a neat, easily retractable foreskin which hid a velvety-soft bulb. Thinking of Julia had made him semi-erect and he stroked his palm soothingly along the length of his shaft, tugging slightly at it as it grew to full hardness.

No, he mustn't waste it, not this time. The thought of being given a chance to make love to a real, experienced woman was too exciting to risk ruining everything by not being able to perform! Greg shuddered at the thought of such humiliation and his cock deflated beneath his hand.

Impatient with himself, he picked up the soap and the bath brush and proceeded to scrub himself thoroughly from head to toe. By the time he stepped out of the bath some fifteen minutes later, he was glowing pinkly all over and his dark hair was plastered, squeaky-clean, to his scalp.

He whistled softly as he towelled himself dry and dressed in newish underwear, clean jeans and a crisp, sky-blue shirt his mother had ironed for him before she left. Peering at himself in the mirror, he lamented the fact that he wouldn't have to shave for a good few days yet before applying aftershave lotion cautiously to his tender skin. The sting made his eyes smart, but the masculine aroma which now swirled around him more than made up for the momentary discomfort.

If only he could see adequately without his glasses, he'd leave them off for tonight. He looked much older without them, he was sure, or perhaps it was just that he could see himself more clearly with them on? Grimacing at himself in the mirror, he combed his hair and fiddled with the buttons on the collar of his shirt.

He'd worn this shirt to the Christmas dinner at the burger bar and Kerry had told him the colour suited him. He flushed at the memory, remembering still the warm glow her small compliment had given him. At the time, all he had managed to mumble in reply was that she looked pretty good herself before scuttling off to find them both another Coke. Pathetic!

Glancing at his watch, Greg saw that it was still only seven o'clock, far too early yet to go upstairs. Pushing all thoughts of Kerry and Julia out of his mind, he switched on his computer and was soon lost in the comforting familiarity of his latest program.

Julia eyed the candles she had put on the table critically, wondering whether she was perhaps being a little too obvious. She didn't want to frighten Greg off completely – she wanted him to relax and enjoy her company.

To that end, she had dressed simply in a plain black dress which quietly played up her curves beneath its high neck and long sleeves. The skirt was short, reaching just past mid-thigh, but there was nothing overtly sexual about it, nothing that screamed 'Mrs Robinson'.

Julia smiled to herself. To hell with worrying about the candles – she'd seen the look in Greg's eyes as he watched her. Only when he thought she wasn't looking, of course, as if she could help but notice the lustful looks he gave her every time he passed near her. There was something very erotic about knowing that one was desired. Erotic and, she had to be honest, very flattering.

The boy was more than ready to lose his virginity and, she had to admit, she was looking forward to relieving him of it. She was surprised at herself, she mused as she took the lasagne she had cooked out of the oven, seducing young men had never particularly appealed to her before. Not that she'd ever really thought about it, if she was truthful. But there was something about Greg, something vulnerable yet inherently strong, which made her look forward to the evening ahead.

There was a knock at her front door and Julia smoothed her hand over her sleek bob before moving to open it.

'Hello!' She smiled widely as she let Greg into the room, noticing that he had bathed and changed since she saw him last. Wrinkling her nose against the brief but overpowering waft of aftershave which preceded him into the room, Julia hid a smile and told him to make himself at home.

'I'm just dishing up, so your timing is perfect!'

She noticed how Greg's gaze took in the candles and the drawn curtains and she saw his Adam's apple bob in his throat. His hair was still damp around his collar and it curled slightly against the stiff fabric.

'I hope you like lasagne?' she asked as she brought the dish to the table.

Conscious that Greg had not, so far, uttered a single word, Julia smiled encouragingly at him. He met her eyes, briefly, before his gaze slid away from hers and he nodded, keeping his eyes downcast.

'It's very kind of you to cook for me,' he mumbled, his cheeks reddening after he'd spoken as if he felt he'd said something crass and foolish.

'Not at all,' Julia said briskly, choosing to ignore his gauche embarrassment. 'I get quite lonely up here on my own at times – it's good to have some company for a change. I've got some wine here – would you uncork it for me?'

She watched from the corner of her eye as Greg struggled manfully with the wine, uttering a secret sigh of relief when she heard the satisfying pop of the cork easing from the neck of the bottle. Greg stood up and poured the wine into the two glasses she had set for them, his smooth-skinned face flushed with success.

'Are you hungry?'

He nodded, then, belatedly remembering his manners, muttered, 'Yes, I am rather.'

Julia dished him up a generous portion and passed him the salad bowl so that he could help himself. It was so quiet she felt that she would hear a pin drop.

'Do you like music?'

'Music? Oh – yes.'

'Anything in particular?'

'What have you got?'

Julia grimaced.

'Nothing especially modern, I'm afraid. Dire Straits, Elton John, Queen. . .'

'Queen would be cool.'

'Greatest Hits?'

'What else?'

He grinned at her for the first time and Julia caught a glimpse of how handsome he would be in a couple of years' time when he'd finally grown into the sharp angles of his face. Turning her back on him, she rummaged through the pile of CDs on the coffee table until she found the one she wanted. The unmistakable voice of Freddie Mercury filled the air as they began to eat and, gradually, Julia felt Greg relax a little across from her.

'I don't know about you, but I'm stuffed!' she groaned when her plate was almost empty.

Greg carried on eating, an appreciative light in his eyes.

'This is the best lasagne I've ever tasted!' he enthused, forgetting, for a moment, to be shy with her.

Julia watched him eat, amused by his enthusiasm.

'I suppose you get to eat more than your fair share of greasy burgers, working at the burger bar on Saturdays?' she suggested.

'Our burgers aren't greasy! Well, not *that* greasy

anyway.' He grinned. 'Kerry always blots hers with a paper towel to dry them off a bit. Only when the manager's not looking, though, or he'd go ballistic.'

'Is Kerry your girlfriend?'

Greg coloured slightly and pushed what remained of his food around his plate with his fork, as if he'd suddenly lost his appetite.

'Not really.'

'But you'd like her to be?' Julia pushed gently.

'She wouldn't want to go out with me!' he blurted suddenly.

'Has she told you that?'

He frowned.

'Of course not! Kerry would never say anything unkind or nasty, she's just not the type.'

'She sounds nice.'

Greg glanced up at her quickly and smiled. He seemed to have lost interest in his food and he pushed his plate aside.

'Yeah, she is nice. And pretty too. Far too good for me.'

'Greg! How can you say such a thing? A fine-looking young man like yourself – surely you have the pick of the girls?'

He shot her an incredulous look.

'Mrs Penn . . . I mean . . . Julia – you have got to be kidding!'

Julia held his eyes for a movement and she saw the way he swallowed, as if his mouth had suddenly grown dry.

'Why don't we sit on the sofa and have some coffee?'

He nodded, his eyes following her every

movement as she rose and picked up their plates.

'I put the percolator on earlier so I only need to pour. You make yourself comfortable, Greg, I'll be back in a minute.'

Greg looked anything but comfortable as he sat self-consciously on the settee and watched Julia walk away. Glancing at him over her shoulder as she reached the door, Julia smiled reassuringly before leaving him alone.

Poor Greg! He really did seem to have a problem with his self-esteem. No wonder Fenella was worried about him. It was a shame too, he wasn't a bad-looking youth at all. If only he wouldn't hold himself as though he wished he was invisible all the time.

Placing two steaming mugs on a tray with a jug of cream and a bowl of sugar, Julia went to join him. Seeing him sitting there, awkwardly folding and unfolding his hands in his lap, she felt a pang of sympathy. Then she saw the tell-tale bulge in the front of his trousers which he was desperately trying to hide from her and she had to dip her head to mask a smile. Her enthusiasm for her 'assignment' was definitely growing the longer the evening went on!

Watching as he sipped his scalding coffee, seeing his tension, Julia took pity on him.

'You don't have to be nervous of me, Greg,' she said, her voice low as she reached across him and took his mug out of his unsteady hands.

'I'm not. . .!'

'Do you like me, Greg?'

He blinked rapidly and Julia gained the distinct impression that he was fighting the urge to leap to his feet, as if he wanted to escape. And yet he didn't want to, the expression in his eyes told her that far more clearly than words ever could.

'Yes – of course I do.'

'But I do make you very nervous, don't I?' She leaned towards him slightly as she spoke, and Greg's eyes flickered over her breasts as they undulated softly under the black jersey of her dress.

'A little,' he admitted, his voice barely more than a husky croak.

'You know, you really do have the most beautiful eyes – do you mind?' she asked him as she reached forward to remove his glasses. 'Can you see without them?'

'A-a bit . . . yes,' he whispered.

'You should try contacts. But then, you wouldn't have your glasses to hide behind, would you?'

'What do you mean?' He shuffled awkwardly in his seat.

'You know what I mean,' Julia smiled slowly, walking her fingers up the button placket of his shirt. 'This is a good colour for you – it brings out the blue of your eyes.'

'Th-thank you. K-K-Kerry liked it. . .' He swallowed hard as Julia ran the soft pad of her forefinger over his trembling lower lip.

'Do you trust me, Greg?' she whispered, sliding her body closer to his on the sofa.

Something sparked in his eyes, a bright, mischievous light which encouraged her.

'No!' he admitted wryly.

Julia grinned.

'Good – you're right not to trust me! My intentions towards you are far from honourable! Do you mind?'

To her relief, Greg responded more actively at last. As if screwing up all his courage, he leaned forward and pressed his lips against hers. For a second, they merely sat there, lips pressed chastely together, then, with a small groan, he put his arms around her and bent her head back so that he could comfortably reach her mouth.

Julia was surprised by the response his kiss invoked in her. Though his technique was far from masterly, what he lacked in expertise he made up for in enthusiasm. She had half expected his lips to be slack and wet, but he kept them firm, moving them on hers as he tasted and teased her lips apart. His tongue was hot and probing and Julia drew it in, swirling her own around it and sucking on it gently.

'Mmm!' she murmured when he finally drew away. 'That was nice! You look hot, Greg . . . wouldn't you be more comfortable if we unbutton your shirt?'

She began to slip the buttons through their buttonholes to reveal his smooth, hairless chest. He was slender, but he had the makings of a good body once he'd finished growing and maybe worked out a little. Julia slipped her hand inside his shirt and pressed her cool palm against his heated flesh.

Greg moistened his dry lips and tried to alter his position to ease the ache caused by his erection.

'Julia. . .?'

'Hmm?' She paused in the exploration of his neck with her lips and looked at him quizzically.

'I . . . why?'

'Why what?'

'Why me?'

She reached up to touch the back of her fingers against his surprisingly strong jawline.

'Why not?'

Greg moved away from her slightly, looking down at her through troubled blue eyes.

'It's just . . . well . . . you're so beautiful Julia. I don't understand why you would want to . . . you know . . . with me.'

He blushed furiously and Julia's heart went out to him. Waiting until he was looking directly at her again, she smiled gently.

'You are a very attractive young man, Greg. I know you don't believe that yet,' she said quickly, placing her fingers against his lips as he began to protest, 'but you will, believe me. Do you want to make love with me?'

Greg gave a great, shuddering sigh, all the answer she needed. Leaning in towards him, Julia kissed him, enfolding her hand over his and guiding it to the generous swell of her breast. She felt his sharp intake of breath as his fingers encountered the hardening crest and an unmistakable tremble ran through his entire body.

It was clear that, while he had obviously had some experience of kissing – with the tantalising Kerry, perhaps – what came next was a mystery to him. Deciding that she would have to guide him, Julia, ran her palms across his shoulders and down his back to rest on his narrow hips before moving slowly to cover the blatant bulge at his groin.

Such a direct approach was obviously too much for him, for his hips jerked involuntarily and his entire body quivered. Greg let his head loll back on to the sofa cushions and groaned with shame. Julia bit her lip, dismayed.

'Oh Greg,' she said after a few minutes, 'I'm sorry. I was going too fast . . . please don't be embarrassed!'

'I must go, I—'

'Go? Oh no, Greg, please don't!'

He paused and looked at her from beneath his lashes.

'You surely don't want me to stay after. . .'

'Of course I do! It's quite natural for a young man of your age, you know. Maybe it's better that it happened like that – now we've got all the time in the world to enjoy ourselves! Look, why don't you take a shower while I clear away the supper things? There's a towelling robe on the back of the door that you can use.'

Greg shot her a grateful glance and disappeared into the bathroom to clean himself up. Julia quickly cleared away the debris from the meal and planned her next move.

It was unfortunate that nature had taken its course so rapidly; the poor boy was obviously mortified. She would have to tread very carefully if his fragile confidence wasn't to be shattered completely.

The most important thing, Julia felt, was that Greg should learn to enjoy a woman's body. Once he had been shown how to please his partner, the rest would come naturally. It would be easier to teach him now that his first youthful rush towards orgasm was over. Hearing the sudden silence in the bathroom as Greg switched off the shower, Julia waited calmly for him to reappear.

She was sitting in the straight-backed chair by the window. The diffused light from the streetlamp outside filtered through the crack between the curtains, creating a golden nebula around her head. As Greg came in, she turned and smiled at him and he felt his heartbeat quicken.

Suddenly he no longer cared quite so much that he had disgraced himself. This beautiful woman was prepared to give him another chance and he was damned if he wasn't going to take it. Moving slowly across the room towards her, Greg was conscious of the softness of her towelling robe against his bare skin. It smelled faintly of her perfume; an intoxicating scent at once both floral and musky which played on his already heightened senses.

She never said a word, merely watching him through those smiling hazel eyes as he approached her. Once he reached her chair, he sank down on to his knees and lay his head in her lap.

'Oh, you beautiful boy,' she whispered as she stroked his hair. 'Come – let me show you what you need to know.'

He needed no further invitation. Taking her outstretched hand, he stood up and allowed her to lead him wordlessly into her bedroom.

Once there, he thrust his hands deep into the

patch pockets of the robe so that she wouldn't see them trembling. Standing very still, he watched as she stepped out of her shoes and kicked them aside. Without her heels she was two or three inches shorter than him and he found he liked the sensation of being larger than her. It brought out a protective instinct he had never realised he possessed. Suddenly it didn't matter that she was so much older and thus so much more experienced than he, the important thing was that they were alone together now in this small room.

His eyes followed the path of her hands as she reached down and hooked her fingers beneath the hem of the plain black dress. Greg held his breath as she drew it slowly upwards, revealing her thighs and then – he could barely believe it – her stocking tops. He'd never seen a real, live woman in stockings and suspenders before and he felt himself grow hard again in response.

This time, though, he knew he would stand some chance of controlling himself and he tried to put the knowledge of his erection to the back of his mind. Julia had rolled her dress up, over the generous swell of her hips to reveal the soft, white skin between her black panties and bra.

Greg discreetly moistened his lips as the creamy globes of her breasts, encased in black lace, came into view. He couldn't take his eyes off them as she raised her arms above her head and pulled the dress over it. The skin stretched taut over the firm flesh for an instant and it was all he could do to stop himself from making a grab for the tantalising mounds which rippled enticingly.

Flinging her dress to one side with careless

abandon, Julia stood before him dressed in nothing but her black bra and panties with their matching suspender belt and sheer, lace-topped stockings. As he watched, she ran her palms slowly down the sides of her breasts before passing them over the neat indentation of her waist and moulding the outward curve of her buttocks. Her hands came to rest on her firm, black-stockinged thighs, and she smiled at him.

'Well, Greg – what do you think?'

Her voice was low and husky and Greg realised for the first time that she was as turned on as he. That knowledge gave him courage and he stepped towards her, reaching out one tentative hand to enclose a breast. Julia moved away from him slightly and she shook her head.

'Lesson number one, Greg – a woman has many more erogenous zones than the obvious.'

Smiling at his bewildered expression, she moved over to the bed and lay back against the pillows which had been piled artistically at the bedhead.

'Come – feel how soft my skin is here. . .'

Reaching for his hand she guided it to the underside of her upper arm and Greg dutifully stroked it. To his surprise, her skin felt like soft, warm velvet. Fascinated, he sat on the bed beside her and began to explore the entire length of her arm with his fingertips. Glancing up at her face, he saw that she had half closed her eyes, clearly enjoying the feeling of his fingers stroking her skin.

Encouraged, he dipped his head and ran his lips lightly along the same path that his fingers

144

had taken, noticing how his action brought little goosebumps up on her skin. Moving up to her neck, he alternately stroked and kissed the long sweep of her throat, gauging her reaction all the while so that he quickly learned how long to go on and how much pressure, or otherwise, to apply.

By the time he progressed to the deep vee between her breasts, Julia was more than ready for him to explore her more sensitive flesh. Tentatively, he smoothed one lacy cup of her bra over her nipple, delighting in the way the whole breast popped out into his hand. He loved the weighty feel of it in his palm, absorbing the silky heat into his own skin as he caressed it.

Far from objecting to what he was sure were his inept fumblings, Julia made herself more comfortable on the pillows, as if settling back to enjoy his attentions rather than merely endure them. Greg watched her face closely as he eased her other breast from the confines of its lacy prison, gratified to see the slight flush of colour seep beneath her skin as he toyed with the hard peak.

Controlling himself with difficulty, he bent his head and placed a small, reverent kiss on each tawny nub. Julia sighed, running her fingers through his hair and thrusting her breasts out sightly, as if she didn't want him to stop. Encouraged, Greg took one quivering breast into his mouth and suckled it. It tasted sweet, the firm, mobile flesh warm against his tongue and he was flooded by a sensation of such extraordinary emotion that it made him tremble.

From her breasts, he bent his head still lower to

nuzzle the gentle curve of her belly. Breathing deeply, he absorbed the scent of her skin and another, more piquant perfume which, he was thrilled to realise, was caused by her arousal.

Remembering with difficulty what she had told him about erogenous zones, Greg bypassed the tantalisingly close mound of her sex, moving instead to caress her legs. It was a revelation to him how a simple stroking action round her ankle bones could provoke such a satisfying response. She pointed her toes, stretching her entire leg, like a cat, and shifting position so that he caught a tempting glimpse of her open crotch.

His fingers trembled as he ran them experimentally up the insides of her calves, pausing to stroke the backs of her knees, then inching towards her stocking tops. The exposed skin of the inside of her thighs was incredibly soft. He could feel the heat emanating from her groin even though her briefs and, at last, he could bear it no longer.

With a muted groan, he buried his face in the hot, damp folds of her crotch, filling his nostrils with her heady feminine perfume. Holding his breath, he raised himself for just long enough to ease the concealing panties down, over her hips and along the length of her legs.

Julia lay very still, her legs slightly apart so that he could see the tender, pink lips of her sex peeking coyly from the dark, curly hair which covered her mons. The whole area was framed by the black suspenders and for a few seconds Greg was content just to look at her. Her skin was so white, so smooth, providing such a contrast to the darkness of her underwear.

Slowly, Greg ran his palms up the front of her thighs, brushing his thumbs along their inside surface until he reached their apex. Then slowly, gently, he ran his thumbs up, along the tender, slightly sticky groove, peeling back the lips of her sex so that he might see inside.

The clear fluid caused by her arousal glistened on the tender pink flesh, inviting him to run his thumbpads back and forth across the swollen flesh. He watched, enthralled, as, at the point where her inner lips joined, a small, shiny button emerged, shyly at first, then more boldly, as if straining towards his fingers.

Greg had never dreamed that a woman's clitoris would be such a distinct, recognisable organ and he was filled with a kind of wondering joy as he touched it for the first time. It was surprisingly hard, moving under his fingers so that he had to recapture it with his thumb.

He didn't need to ask Julia if he was doing it right, she had almost closed her eyes and he could see a faint sheen of perspiration pushing its way through the pores of her upper lip. Impulsively, he bent his head and licked it away, revelling in the salty taste on his tongue.

Hearing her small gasp, he threw caution to the wind and bent his head so that he could press a little kiss against the shiny, hard bud which he was holding between his fingers.

His own action took him by surprise; never in his wildest dreams had he ever dreamt that he would be overcome by the urge to kiss and suck a woman's pussy. Once he had tasted her, though, he didn't want to move away.

147

Her love juices were unexpectedly sweet, coating his lips and tongue with a clear fluid the texture of honey. Acting on instinct, he darted his tongue into the deep well of her body, drawing more fluid up and along the heated channels either side of her labia.

Jabbing his tongue quickly against her clitoris, he nuzzled the fragrant folds of her flesh and closed his teeth gently over the now quivering bud. To his surprise, Julia's response was both instantaneous and devastatingly uninhibited. Her hips bucked so that his face was crushed against her vulva and the core of her vibrated violently against his tongue. Lashing the small button with the flat of his tongue, Greg drew every last drop of love-dew from her, kissing her labia in reluctant farewell as she, at last, sank back down on the bed, apparently exhausted.

He raised his head and looked at Julia, unable to hide his exultation. She laughed throatily at the look of triumph in his eyes and slowly widened her legs.

'Now, Greg darling – make love to me?'

He shrugged off the towelling robe and knelt on the bed, between her knees. His penis, fully restored to potency now, reared up, like a flagstaff, between his legs. Taking the condom she passed him without a word, he rolled it carefully over his engorged shaft before positioning himself at the entrance to her body.

His heartbeat quickened as the realisation of what he was about to do hit him. His pride that he had been able to make her come gave him courage, spurring him on. Bracing his hands either side of her head, he swallowed hard as she reached down and guided him in. Then he sank into her, feeling the hot, pulpy flesh of her labia draw him into the tight passage.

'Oh God, oh God!' he whispered as he began to move inside her.

He had always believed it would be good, but nothing had prepared him for the utter bliss of the actual act. With every outward stroke, the walls of her vagina seemed to clutch at him, creating the most exquisite sensations all along the length of his shaft.

Breaking out into a sweat all over, he began to move faster, pumping his slim hips up and down as he began the dizzy upward spiral towards release.

He cried out as he came, feeling his seed gushing in harsh, almost violent spurts before he collapsed over her, welcoming the feel of her arms coming around his body. He felt over-whelmed, love, gratitude and wonder mixing in him until he could not say *how* he felt.

'Thank you,' he whispered, his lips moving over her hair. 'Oh Julia – thank you so much.'

Julia stroked his hair, running her palms soothingly over his shoulders and down his back, making loving noises. He had surprised her – she hadn't expected him to be able to bring her to orgasm with his lips and tongue like that. His wonder, his transparent gratitude to her was touching and she was surprised to feel herself perilously close to tears. To hide them, she eased him gently away.

He disappeared briefly into the bathroom before coming back to slip between the sheets with her. She smiled at his innocent assumption that she would want him to stay, surprised to realise that she did. Closing her eyes, she allowed him to draw her close, liking the feel of his strong young arms encircling her shoulders.

'That was . . . incredible!' he whispered after a few minutes.

'It was, wasn't it? Greg? Will you do something for me tomorrow?'

'Anything.'

'Ask Kerry for a date.'

She felt him stiffen slightly beside her, and she wondered if he had thought would be more between them than this brief interlude. He was silent for a few minutes, than he nodded.

'Yes, I think I will.'

Looking up at him, Julia caught his eye and saw that he understood perfectly that this was to be the extent of the relationship between the two of them. To her relief, he did not appear to be hurt by the realisation. She kissed him, gently, on the cheek.

'Go to sleep now,' she whispered.

He returned her smile, then closed his eyes. Within minutes he was asleep, a contented smile playing around the corners of his mouth.

Chapter Nine

GAVIN WAS PHILOSOPHICAL about Julia's decision not to go back to college.

'If it's not for you, Mum, then that's fair enough. At least you've looked into it, so you can make an informed choice. So – what *are* you going to do?'

Julia sighed heavily.

'Have you seen your father lately?' she asked.

'I called round earlier in the week.'

'How was he?'

Gavin shrugged his shoulders.

'A bit shell-shocked, I suppose, but he's surviving. He wants you to go home, you know.'

'Did he tell you that?'

'Not in so many words. We men sense these things.'

Julia laughed and threw a cushion at him which he dodged with ease.

'You do think I've done the right thing, don't you Gavin?'

'Do you?'

Julia sighed again.

'Some days I think yes, others. . .' She shrugged.

'Come on, Mum – give yourself time. No one walks away from a twenty-year-old marriage, no matter how dreary, without some regrets, surely?'

Julia smiled affectionately at him. How had this great strapping son of hers become so wise?'

'I'm seeing Nick again,' she confided impulsively.

'I know. Go on Mum – go for it! You've only got one life, you know!'

Gavin's words echoed in Julia's head as she dressed to meet Nick the following Thursday. He was probably right – the fourteen-year age gap between them would only be a problem if she made it into one. Nick seemed to have no qualms about the fact that she was older than him, and she had to admit, with him she had enjoyed the best sex she'd experienced in ages!

Downstairs, she bumped into Greg coming through the front door. There was a small, red-haired girl with elfin features and a happy smile holding his hand. She could, Julia guessed, only be Kerry.

'Hi Greg!'

'Hello Julia.' He grinned fondly at her and she remembered how he had left her bed the previous Sunday morning, full of the joys of spring. Any fears she had had that he would be unable to accept the bounds she had set on their relationship proved groundless as he had dressed.

'You know,' he had said, reaching across the bed to kiss her, 'I've been thinking about what you said before. About Kerry. I *will* ask her out – I'm sure she likes me and I'll be a much better friend to her now I feel better about myself.'

And now here he was, clearly having been successful in his aim and pleased as punch with himself for having dared.

'I'd like you to meet Kerry—' He presented the girl as if she was some rare and beautiful object and Julia shook her hand. 'Kerry, this is Julia, our lodger.' He caught Julia's eye and winked at her mischievously.

'Pleased to meet you!' The girl gave her a happy smile and the pair of them ran up the stairs to Greg's room.

Julia stood in the hallway and watched until they were out of sight, marvelling at the change in Greg. Gone was the 'don't-notice-me' stoop of his shoulders and the habitual avoidance of everyone's eyes. The young man running up the stairs with his girlfriend was tall and proud, confident in a way that he had never been until he had discovered that his own body could be his best friend.

'Quite a change, isn't it?'

Julia jumped as Fenella called softly to her from across the hall. She had been so wrapped up in watching Greg that she hadn't noticed the other woman emerge from the studio. Julia smiled at her.

'Isn't it just! I have a feeling that Greg's computer will be badly neglected from now on!'

Fenella chuckled.

'That's no bad thing! It's wonderful to see him so happy, and with a girlfriend of his own at last! By the way, I never did thank you for looking after him last weekend.'

Their eyes met across the hallway and Julia silently acknowledged that they would never speak of the role she had played in helping Greg find his self-confidence.

'It was my pleasure,' she replied sincerely. 'Really, he was no trouble at all!'

She left the house with a light heart, glad that her tutoring of Greg had borne fruit so quickly.

Nick was waiting for her and Julia looked around his flat with interest. It was modern and very clean. The furniture, though sparse, was practical and new, tubular black with a grey carpet enlivened with a bright red patterned dhurrie rug. There was music playing on the stereo, a strange, inherently tuneless sound which gave the room an almost surreal atmosphere.

'Something smells delicious!' she told him as he came over to kiss her.

'Are you hungry?'

'Mmm! Are you?'

He nuzzled her neck, nipping her earlobe gently before moving away.

'First we eat – then. . .' He laughed softly and disappeared into the kitchen. 'Make yourself at home,' he called, his disembodied voice sounding far away.

Julia took off her jacket and shoes and sat down on the sofa. It was unexpectedly comfortable, given the thinness of the cushions and she drew her feet up beneath her and picked up one of Nick's cookery books.

It was warm in the flat and welcoming with its three red uplighters illuminating the corners of the room and casting shadows across the dim centre. After a few minutes, Julia put the book down and leaned her head back against the cushions.

'Asleep already?' Nick teased when he joined her.

Julia opened her eyes and smiled up at him, taking the tray he was offering her and tucking into the spicy Indian dish he had prepared. It was delicious and she told him so, earning herself one of his endearing, slightly lopsided grins.

'I'm glad you liked it. I've got you something just a little bit different for afters . . . in a while.'

Intrigued, Julia watched him as he cleared away their plates before joining her on the sofa. His lips were urgent as he pressed them down on hers and Julia found herself responding to the swift flare of passion she sensed in him. Though his body was becoming more familiar to her, he still had the power to surprise and delight her and she welcomed the weight of his hand against her breast as he caressed her, happy for him to take her quickly, as he had before.

He did not take her, though, instead he produced a red silk scarf from behind the cushions and rubbed it sensuously across her cheek.

'Will you let me blindfold you?'

Julia blinked in surprise, as much at his urgent, husky tone as at his unexpected request.

'We-ell. . .'

She had never been blindfolded before and for

155

some reason the idea rather frightened her. As if sensing her misgivings, Nick kissed her face, pressing butterfly kisses on her eyelids and running his hands urgently over the upper half of her body.

'You'll be quite safe,' he whispered. 'I won't tie your hands, so you can take it off any time you want to.'

That sounded more comfortable, and Julia relaxed a little.

'But why?' she asked him, feeling slightly foolish.

He smiled at her and kissed the tip of her nose.

'I want to play a game with you.'

'A game?'

'Yes. I want you to guess what I've made for you to eat.'

Gradually, Julia understood.

'You mean . . . like a tasting game?'

'Something like that. Will you try it?'

She stared into his eyes. They were not calm now, but a stormy, sexy grey and Julia felt a little thrill of anticipation run up her spine.

'All right,' she whispered.

The silk felt cool against her temples as he tied the scarf around her eyes.

'Comfortable?' he whispered.

Julia nodded, straining to see through the thin fabric, but all she could see was a shimmering red glow.

'Do you mind if I take off your skirt and blouse?'

She raised her head, alarmed.

'Why?'

'Because I like looking at you in your underwear. Will you indulge me?'

Julia's lips trembled slightly as she nodded, aware that her entire body was alert, bristling with anticipation. To her surprise, she found she rather liked the sense of danger engendered by wearing the blindfold and she allowed herself to relax as Nick slowly unfastened the buttons of her blouse.

She was wearing a simple white bra, suspender and brief set with white, lacy-topped stockings. As Nick eased her blouse over her shoulders, the air brushed her skin, causing her nipples to rise and harden. She trembled as he removed her skirt and she was left in her underwear.

'Are . . . are you looking at me?' she asked, aware of his eyes on her bare skin.

'Of course,' he said throatily. 'You are so, so beautiful, Julia . . . don't look so worried – relax.'

His hands smoothed soothingly down the fronts of her thighs before moving up to brush her collarbone and caress her neck.

'Trust me – you're going to enjoy this.'

Julia turned her face towards the sound of his soft footfall as he disappeared into the kitchen. He was wearing jeans and a black T-shirt, but his feet were bare, so they made little noise. He seemed to Julia to be gone a long time. She felt horribly vulnerable, sitting in a strange room in her underwear, blindfolded. She didn't quite know what to do, so she simply sat quietly, her hands folded in her lap, and waited.

'Here we are.'

She breathed a sigh of relief as Nick returned

and she heard the clink of plates and cutlery being placed on the low, glass-topped coffee table beside the sofa.

'Try this.'

He held a spoon near her mouth and she smelled the sharp tang of limes.

'What is it?' she asked suspiciously.

'You have to guess,' he reminded her, patiently.

Reluctantly, Julia opened her mouth to allow him to insert the spoon. The food was cold and slippery.

'Lime jelly?'

'That's right!' He sounded pleased. 'One point to you! Now this – careful, you'll need to chew it.'

'Peanut butter!' Julia said, making a face. She hated peanuts.

She gasped as Nick's tongue rasped along the inside of her lower lip before he gave her something to take the nutty taste away.

'Mmm! Crushed strawberries . . . and cream – oh!'

She cried out as the cool, viscous liquid dripped into her cleavage and ran slowly down between her breasts.

'Sorry,' Nick murmured thickly, dabbing at it with his tongue before moving up to kiss her mouth.

Julia could taste the cream on his tongue and swirled her own around it, offering him the lingering taste of the strawberries. She could not imagine why, but the game was causing a deep, pulsing throb to beat in the secret places between her legs. Already she could feel her labia swell and moisten and her nipples strained against the restrictive fabric of her bra.

'Ready for some more?' Nick's voice was husky, as if he too felt the erotic charge which was travelling through her body. Julia nodded, unable to trust herself to speak.

He fed her icing sugar, followed by stewed apple so tart it made her eyes water behind the blindfold. This was followed by a spoonful of rich chocolate mousse which slipped down her throat, coating it with sweetness.

'Mmm – you like that, don't you?' Nick whispered, close to her ear.

Julia nodded, reaching up blindly to touch his face. He turned his head and captured the tip of her little finger between his lips, sucking gently on it before easing her back on the cushions.

'This bra looks uncomfortable – do you mind if I take it off?'

Julia nodded wordlessly, unable to understand why she had been yearning for him to do just that. The music, soft and continuous, swirled around her head, lending a sense of unreality to the situation which she found strangely erotic.

She gasped as he pressed the back of one cold teaspoon against her burgeoning nipples, one after the other. Opening her mouth in anticipation when she heard the clink of a metal spoon against china, Julia was unprepared for the sudden, shockingly cold application of lime-flavoured jelly to her quivering breasts.

'Nick. . .!'

'Hush! I'm going to rub it in – this kind of massage therapy would cost you a fortune on a

159

health farm!'

She had no doubt it would and she closed her eyes behind the blindfold, enjoying the sensation of the cool, slippery jelly being rubbed into her heated skin. Next he dribbled something into her navel ... cream she guessed. Her stomach muscles contracted involuntarily as she felt his tongue lap at it, dipping into her navel and tasting the sticky cream.

She did not object when his fingers hooked into the waistband of her panties and he drew them down, over her hips and along her legs, leaving her dressed in nothing but her white suspender belt and lacy-topped white stockings.

'God, Julia,' he breathed, 'if you could only see yourself ... I know! I have a Polaroid camera – would you like me to take some photographs for you to enjoy later?'

Julia's protest was half-hearted for she had to admit that the idea of being photographed in such a compromising position turned her on. She sensed Nick leave the room, then return. She heard the click of the camera, then he put it aside and lay his hand on the lower part of her belly.

'Do you trust me, Julia?' he asked her, his voice low.

'Yes,' she whispered, conscious that her throat had grown dry and her legs were beginning to tremble with anticipation.

'Then spread your legs for me.'

His words were a shock, yet she found herself edging her feet slowly apart until one hung over the edge of the sofa and the other stretched along its length.

'That's it,' he breathed, and Julia heard the quiet click of the camera again.

Her breath began to hurt in her chest as she breathed shallowly, trying to anticipate his next move. She sensed his eyes on her and she wetted her dry lips with the tip of her tongue, wishing she could see him, but knowing that she would not be half so aroused if she could.

'I've been working on a new recipe,' he said suddenly and she sensed that he had turned his attention to the table. 'I call it honey-glazed strawberries with cream.'

Julia gasped as she felt the first, shocking drop of honey drip with unerring accuracy on to the soft skin of her labia.

'Oh Nick . . . Nick, I don't know. . .'

He bent forward and kissed her on the lips.

'Don't bottle out now, my love – the best is yet to come!'

He smeared the honey around her vulva, massaging it in and allowing it to mingle with the moisture produced by her own body. Julia could feel her body open out, like a flower drinking in the sun, and she trembled violently.

'Ssh!' Nick soothed her, kissing her neck and breasts and stroking the hair away from her face with the palm of his hand. 'There's nothing to worry about, nothing at all. . .'

He kissed a path down her body, between her breasts and over her abdomen, sticky now with the drying cream. Once he reached the apex of her thighs, he rested her cheek against the soft mound of her belly and watched his fingers dabbling in the swollen folds of her sex.

'More honey, I think . . . and a little cream. . .'

The fluids combined as he rubbed them in and Julia felt her clitoris stir and thrust itself out, demanding attention. Seeing what was happening, Nick swirled his finger slowly round the hardening nub until Julia began to gasp. The sensation was exquisite, though he stopped just before it was able to build to a climax.

'Patience,' he admonished when she let out a groan of disappointment, 'I haven't finished yet!' He rested the whole of his hand over her sticky quim, as if keeping it warm while he reached for a plate he had placed by the side of the sofa. 'The main ingredient of my recipe is sweet, ripe, hulled strawberries, like the ones I have here. Now . . . where do you think these should go?'

As she realised what he intended, Julia was paralysed with shock and . . . to her dismay, an indescribable yearning.

'Oh yes!' she heard her own voice breathe, as if from far away.

Nick chuckled softly and bent to kiss her softly opened lips.

'Would you like to try a strawberry? Here – I'll dip this one in sugar, then cream. . .'

He pressed the strawberry gently against her teeth and Julia let it slip over her tongue. She sucked it slowly, enjoying the sensation of the pulpy fruit coating her tongue and throat.

She gasped as she felt Nick press another one against the entrance to her vagina. Surely he wasn't really going to insert it? He did, pushing it high up her with his middle finger. Despite herself, Julia squirmed on his finger, wanting more.

He did not disappoint her. A second strawberry was pressed gently inside her, then another and another until her moisture-slick sheath was full of the ripe fruit. She could feel it oozing from her, mixing with the concoction of honey and cream he had rubbed into her earlier.

'Does that feel good?' he murmured, close to her ear.

She muttered incoherently, shame fighting against her overwhelming need to widen her legs and thrust her pelvis up towards his stroking fingers.

Nick kissed her face again, then kissed and licked a path down her body until he was at eye-level with her strawberry-filled passage.

'Oh Julia,' he whispered with a break in his voice, 'it's all seeping out of you. . .'

He bent his head and Julia felt the kiss of his lips and tongue as he began to nibble gently at the gooey concoction oozing from her body. Murmuring small, appreciative noises, he licked around her honey-and-cream-smeared vulva before going back to suck the strawberries into his mouth.

As the last of the strawberries slipped out of her, Julia experienced the most incredible sense of letting go and she whimpered, desperate for release. Seeing she had reached the limit of her endurance, Nick lapped at her labia with strong, firm strokes, swirling his tongue around her sticky clit until she cried out for him to stop as the sensation became too much. The music seemed to reach a loud, discordant crescendo just as the waves crashed over her, making her head swim

163

as she arched her back and threw her legs as wide as they could go before scissoring them back and forth, wanting to prolong the sensation for as long as possible.

She clutched him to her as she came, tears seeping from beneath her blindfold as she was overcome by the strength of it. Nick eased it gently from her eyes so that she could see the expression on his face. It was at once triumphant and adoring and Julia welcomed the swift thrust of his body as he entered her.

His face was smeared with strawberry juice and cream and honey and the sweet, heavy dew of her body. Julia held his face between her hands and licked the cream, tasting herself on his skin. Thrusting urgently into her willing body, Nick raced towards his own release, crushing Julia's mouth under his as he came.

They lay, joined together, for a long time. The music had stopped and the silence had that heavy, velvety quality which Julia loved. Nick seemed to be as content as she, to remain as they were but, inevitably, they eventually had to part. The dried honey and cream, combined with the perspiration from their bodies had stuck them together and they peeled apart loudly, laughing.

'A bath, I think,' Nick suggested. 'No, you lie there,' he said as she made to get up. 'I'll run you a bath and you can contemplate just how beautiful you really are.'

He handed the two Polaroid pictures he had snapped and Julia pressed her fingers against her lips to hold in the gasp which rose to her lips. She hardly recognised herself in the wildly abandoned woman in the red silk blindfold who lay, legs akimbo, on Nick's sofa. Her breasts were swollen and thrust out, her clearly visible labia moist and open, waiting. . .

Embarrassed, suddenly, she tore the photographs into little pieces, looking up guiltily as Nick came back into the room and caught her.

He raised his eyebrows when he saw what she had done, but he didn't say a word, merely taking the pieces from her and dropping them into the wastepaper basket. Then he came over to the sofa and crouched down beside her, unselfconscious as always in his nakedness.

'I'm sorry,' she whispered, regretting already her impulsive reaction.

'It doesn't matter. Tell me, though – did you enjoy having the photos taken at the time?'

Julia dropped her eyes and nodded. Nick lifted her chin with his forefinger and made her look at him.

'That's all that matters. A little bit of shame is . . . exciting, don't you think?'

Julia did not reply, and he smiled.

'Come on – there's a hot, soapy bath waiting for you.'

In the bathroom, he took off what remained of her clothes and she climbed into the bath. Nick wouldn't let her do a thing, all that was that was required of her was for her to lie back in the water and relax. He used a big, soft sponge to soap her, first her arms and her legs, then the rest of her body, seeking out all the nooks and crannies which might have retained a trace of his strawberry, honey and cream dessert.

It was wonderfully soothing to be bathed by someone else, and by the time Nick had finished, Julia was almost asleep. He half lifted her out of the water and wrapped her in a towel before jumping into her water and quickly sluicing himself down.

Julia stood like an automaton as he dried her and slipped a baggy white T-shirt over her head. She felt unutterably tired and she was glad Nick had made the decision for her that she was staying the night. The T-shirt was soft from countless launderings and smelled faintly of Nick. Julia rubbed her cheek across the shoulder and leaned against him, unable to keep her eyes open for another moment.

Vaguely, she was aware of Nick guiding her through to the bedroom and of sinking down on to cool, fresh sheets. Then a duvet was tucked around her chin and Nick's warm, naked body slipped in beside her.

She thought he said, 'Sleep well, my love,' but she couldn't be sure. Within minutes, she was fast asleep.

Chapter Ten

WAKING IN NICK'S arms the following morning, Julia sensed a subtle shift in their relationship. He had never allowed her the upper hand in bed that she had enjoyed with Paul and Greg, and latterly with Michael, but not until last night had he demonstrated so clearly how much he enjoyed taking charge. Though easy going during the rest of the day, Nick was clearly a man who liked to be in control in the bedroom. And yet everything he did he did with such good humour, and he had never treated her with anything but respect. Even last night.

'Hello.'

He opened his eyes and smiled up at her.

He didn't ask her why she was propped up on one elbow, staring at him, he simply accepted that she was. It was obvious that it didn't bother him, he had no secrets to hide. Julia traced a line down the middle of his face with her forefinger, pressing her finger pad gently against his closed lips. Nick kissed her fingertip and his lips curved into a smile.

Stretching languorously, Julia was unprepared for the grab he made for her waist and she squealed as he brought her down on to the pillows beside him. Laughing, he pinned her down with his upper body, capturing her wrists and holding them above her head, exposing her naked breasts to his lazy gaze.

Suddenly he was no longer laughing and Julia sucked in her breath as she saw the way his eyes had darkened. She gasped as he dipped his head to kiss first one breast, then the other, his lips hard and cool against her sleep-warmed flesh.

His beard, pushing relentlessly through on his jaw, scraped her skin and she shivered, aware of the slow wakening and unfolding of the sleeping flesh between her legs. They didn't need words, Nick was so attuned to her feelings that he knew the moment when she surrendered to him and kissed her, hard.

Julia clutched at his shoulders, her head spinning as his tongue plundered her mouth and his fingers sought and found the centre of her arousal. She murmured restlessly against his lips as he extracted a brief, shockingly sudden orgasm from her before slipping inside her.

He made love to her slowly, leisurely, his long, wavy blond hair slipping forward over his face as he moved in and out of her body. Julia watched his face, eager to catch every nuance of his expression as his breathing became shallow and his skin began to glow.

It was bliss, coming together with him like this

and Julia knew that there was nowhere else in the world she would rather be on a Friday morning than here, in bed with Nick. Thank God it was not her responsibility to open the coffee shop today for she knew that, for once in her life, pleasure would take precedence over duty.

She clutched him to her as he spilled his seed into her welcoming body and they rolled together into a more comfortable position. After a while, he smiled at her and, resting his head in one hand, he raised himself up slightly and studied her as she had him earlier.

'Why don't you move in here, with me?' he said suddenly.

Julia could not have been more shocked if he had suggested she dance naked through the House of Commons on a wet Tuesday.

'I already have a perfectly adequate flat, thank you,' she said lightly, unsure as to how she should reply.

'I know. But I like waking up to find your face on the pillow next to mine. We're good together, you and me.'

Julia could not deny that, but she shook her head.

'I'm very fond of you, Nick,' she said carefully, 'but I'm not ready to take a step like moving in together. It's far too soon.'

He shrugged, pushing impatiently at the hair which fell across his eyes.

'Are you?' he asked.

'Am I what?'

'Fond of me?'

Julia dropped her eyes.

'Of course.'

'You don't think that fondness might, well – grow into something . . . more lasting?'

Julia's head was spinning at the unexpected turn the conversation had taken.

'Nick . . . it wouldn't work.'

He frowned heavily.

'Why the hell not?'

'Well, for a start, I'm a good deal older than you—'

'Fourteen years and three months. Nothing at all, really. Why are you so hung up on age?'

'I'm not! You're the one who's worked out the difference down to the last month!'

He went on as if she'd never spoken.

'I mean – you take care of yourself, you're as beautiful as you ever were when you were younger. . .'

Julia laughed cynically.

'Come off it, Nick – you can't deny that time comes between us. Gravity is already taking its toll on my body and you can't tell me that you'd honestly prefer sags and bags and stretch marks to the firm young flesh of a woman your own age.'

'I'm not interested in "women my age",' he said, his tone measured, 'I'm interested in you. These marks,' he stroked his fingertip lightly along one of the silvery tracks on her stomach, 'they show you've lived. They're not ugly or off-putting. Girls my age see a guy more than once and want "a relationship", then wonder why the guy runs a mile. You've done all that – I know you come to me because you want *me*, Nick

Lowther, not what I represent.'

Julia shook her head.

'Fine words, Nick, but aren't you as bad as those girls you're so quick to dismiss? You and I have made love a few times and you automatically move to stake your claim on me, mark me as your own exclusive territory.'

Nick stared at her silently for several seconds.

'*Touché*,' he said quietly, his voice dropping huskily as he asked her, 'Is that the way you see it?'

'Yes. No. Oh, I don't know! I just know it wouldn't work. I've done the marriage and children bit – you haven't. You should be on the lookout for a girl who can share all that with you. Now stop it!' She frowned as he began to argue again. 'Don't spoil things, Nick. Just enjoy what we've got and take each day as it comes. Please?'

He reached across to cup her cheek with his palm and his lips brushed her temple in a tender caress.

'All right.'

'No more talk about me moving in with you?'

'No. Satisfied?' He had an amused glint in his eye which Julia didn't quite trust.

'Hmm. Are you going to do the gentlemanly thing now and drive me home? Or do I have to call a taxi?'

Nick was quiet on the drive back to her flat. As he drew up outside and switched off the engine, he turned to her, an uncharacteristically solemn expression on his face.

'Am I forgiven yet?'

Julia blew the air between her teeth in an expression of exasperation.

'Idiot! Of course.' She leaned over to kiss him on the lips and he closed his eyes for a second.

'I don't want to lose you.' He smiled then and his whole face changed. 'Come on – I'll accept a coffee in payment for the ride home!'

Upstairs there were several letters waiting for Julia, one of which was from Melissa. Nick took over in the kitchen while Julia read it.

'She's settling in all right and she wants me to go up for Parent Orientation Day – whatever that is! At least Mel's speaking to me again – she hasn't replied to any of my letters and I was beginning to think she was never going to forgive me for leaving her dad!'

'I told you she'd come round,' Nick said, passing her a mug of instant. 'Will you go with Michael?'

Trying to ignore the slight petulance in his tone which she could tell he was trying very hard to control, Julia scanned the letter again.

'Oh no – it's tomorrow! That's typical of Melissa; she must have known about this before. Michael is away on a field trip with year eight at school. Don't you look so pleased – that means I'll have to spend half the day travelling up by train.'

'I'll drive you.'

Julia looked at him, surprised by his offer.

'It wouldn't be much fun for you, Nick. It's a long way and once we get there there won't be much for you to do.'

'I'd like to come. The weather forecast is good – we could set off early and stop for lunch on the way. Maybe we could take a picnic.'

'All right. You provide the transport and I'll

bring the picnic. But you're going to have to go now, I've got to get ready to go to the coffee shop.'

'Okay. I'll pick you up at nine in the morning.'

Julia was subdued as the miles were eaten up by their passage along the motorway. Nick left her to her own thoughts until they had turned off, heading cross-country, before saying, 'Is there something wrong?'

Julia sighed heavily, forcing her attention outwards, away from her troubled thoughts.

'I'm sorry, Nick; I was miles away.'

'I noticed. So what's up?'

'The coffee shop is closing down.'

'What? When?'

'At the end of November. I get the impression that the owners don't want to sell, but business isn't good and they just don't have the capital needed to build it up.'

'Couldn't they go to the bank for help?'

'I suppose so. But they're both elderly – I think they feel the time has come to call it a day and the decrease in business has simply given them the push they were waiting for.

'So where does that leave you?'

Julia grimaced.

'Out of work, I suppose.'

Nick was silent for a while as he found the picnic spot they had decided on earlier. Pulling into a layby, he switched off the engine and they both stepped out into the bright autumn sunshine.

'Is this the place?'

Julia nodded.

'Over that gate and along the bridleway. If I

remember rightly there's a lovely little dell there. We stopped here when we brought Melissa up for her interview at the university.'

Sure enough, after a pleasant few minutes' walk they came to a clearing of lush, bright green grass, sheltered by a long sweep of trees, their leaves glowing gold in the sunlight. Nick looked around approvingly before spreading the blanket on the ground and flopping down on to his stomach. Reaching his arms up, over his head, he stretched out his shoulder muscles before folding his arms and resting his cheek on them.

He watched Julia through half-closed eyes as she lay down on her back and bent her elbow over her eyes against the glare of the sun.

'Mmm, this is lovely,' she breathed, settling her body more comfortably on the blanket and letting out her breath on a long, contented sigh.

Nick reached across the short gap separating them and laid his hand gently on her stomach, not moving it, simply allowing it to rest there. Though apparently casual, it was an intensely intimate gesture which spread warmth right through her belly to the tops of her thighs.

Turning her head slightly so that she could look at him, Julia marvelled at how much she desired him still. When they had started their affair, she had genuinely thought that after they had made love once, the need would have left her system, rather like it had when she had gone home with Paul. Nick was different, though. Every time they made love it seemed to increase rather then diminish her hunger for him.

Looking at him now, lying relaxed beside her

on the blanket, his long hair loose, glinting gold in the sunlight, she felt a lump rise in her throat. Impulsively, she rolled on to her side and ran the backs of her fingers tenderly down the side of his face, before leaning over to brush her lips softly over his.

Drawing back slightly, she saw he was watching her quizzically, his clear grey eyes calm and almost guileless as he raised his eyebrows.

'What is it?' he asked softly.

Julia smiled slightly and drew back, feeling embarrassed.

'Nothing . . . it's nothing.' She shook her head, avoiding his eyes. How could she begin to articulate the feelings which had just taken her by surprise?

Nick seemed to understand. His lips curving into the gentlest of smiles, he drew her back down on to the blanket, tucking her head into the space between his head and his shoulder and kissing her lightly on the hair.

Julia closed her eyes, savouring the moment. Nick's arms were strong around her body, yet she knew he would not try to stop her if she drew away. That freedom made her want to stay where she was, safe in his embrace. She was glad that he hadn't misinterpreted her actions earlier and tried to make a pass at her. At this moment, she didn't want sex, she wanted intimacy, pure and simple, and he seemed perfectly content to share that need with her.

They lay like that, comfortably entwined for some time. Drowsing lazily in the lukewarm sunlight, they enjoyed the brief oasis of peace in the middle of a potentially hectic day. Somewhere nearby a farmer was chugging up and down his fields in his tractor. Traffic could be heard faintly, in the distance, but nothing intruded directly into their peace.

Julia wriggled slightly as, after a while, she felt Nick's hand begin to move slowly up and down her side, brushing the underside of her breast and polishing her hipbone. Turning sleepily in his arms, she pressed herself against the lean, hard length of his body and enjoyed, for a moment, the feel of it against hers.

His heart beat steadily against the palm of her hand and she rested it there for a moment before sliding it across his chest. His skin was warm beneath the white and navy striped T-shirt, his nipples responding instantly to the light brush of her fingertips. Julia circled the hardening nubs lightly with her fingernail, first one, then the other, smiling when he craned his neck to nibble at her earlobe in response.

Moving out of his reach, she moulded the well-defined contours of his chest before sliding her hand lower to caress his abdomen. His muscles tightened as her fingers strayed lower, his stomach pulling in, creating a gentle dip which she could not resist stroking. Nick closed his eyes as she rubbed rhythmically back and forth over his belly, circling his navel and edging steadily closer to the waistband of his jeans.

Julia could sense his excitement, could see it in the way his thighs tensed and the way his lips parted to let his breath escape at an increasingly rapid, shallow pace. Leaning over him, she kissed

176

the corner of his mouth, then traced the line where his lips met with the very tip of her tongue.

She loved the taste of him, so familiar, so very male and she could feel the tendrils of arousal creeping slowly, deliciously, through her limbs, centring in the pit of her stomach. Shifting her position slightly, she ran her hand down the hard muscle of his thigh and back up again, brushing the backs of her fingers teasingly over the unmistakable bulge caged behind the button fastening of his jeans.

'Julia. . .' he whispered.

'Nick. Lie still – let go.'

Her words brushed over his lips as she bent down to kiss him. He accepted the kiss passively, opening his lips under hers to allow her tongue access to the wet, warm cavern of his mouth. Her tongue probed the sensitive insides of his cheeks, drawing the sweetness of his breath from him, stoking her own desire.

Sitting back on her heels, she was aware of the moisture which was seeping into her plain cotton panties and she stood up, towering over him. Nick watched through narrowed eyes as she lifted her skirt and eased her knickers down, over her hips and thighs, letting them drop to the ground. She noticed how he moistened his lips, as if they had suddenly grown dry and she felt a surge of secret, feminine power.

Kicking the panties aside, she smiled as a gust of wind blew up her skirt and treated Nick to a glimpse of her naked sex beneath the demure dress she was wearing. Kneeling down with one knee either side of his thighs, she ran both hands up his legs, allowing them to meet at his groin.

Nick sighed raggedly as she began to trace the line of his erection, up and down and up and down.

'Julia – please!'

That was what she had been waiting to hear; just a small plea, a tangible sign of his need for her. In response, she ran her fingertips tantalisingly round the inside of his waistband before pulling his T-shirt loose. Exposing a small circle of firm, lightly furred flesh, she bent her head and kissed him, just below his navel.

She could smell the unmistakable scent of sex on him, musky and slightly sharp and her own sex-flesh fluttered in response to the stimulus. Her own breath came more shallowly now, and she could feel a trickle of sweat running between her breasts.

Unfastening the top button of his fly, Julia noted that Nick swallowed hard, his hands clenching into fists, as if he was struggling to keep them passive by his sides. It was like opening a new box of chocolates, this slow drawing apart of his jeans and Julia licked her lips in anticipation.

Underneath he was wearing plain white cotton boxer shorts, the thin material straining against his erection. Slipping the single button through its anchor, Julia slipped her hand inside his shorts and caressed the silky-soft skin of the tumescent rod. Grasping it gently, she brought it out and ran her hand up and down its length. The loose skin moved easily against the hard centre and her hand quickly became slippy with the clear fluid which seeped from its end.

Impulsively, she bent her head to kiss the velvety glans, running her tongue along the groove and lapping at his juices. Nick groaned, his hand reaching for her head. He stroked her hair, cupping her cheek and urging her to stop before she pushed him past the point of no return.

Taking pity on him, Julia knelt up. The coarse grass scratched slightly at her knees, the longer blades tickling her thighs. Hitching her full skirt around her waist, she positioned herself over him. She wanted him to be able to see his penis disappearing into the moist, heated entrance to her body.

She shivered as his cock-head nudged her labia and the soft inner lips opened to welcome him. With a gasp, she sank down on him, enclosing him, drawing him so deeply inside her that she could feel the taut, hair-roughened skin of his balls scrape against the stretched, tender flesh of her perineum.

Sitting quite, quite still, Julia reached down and touched the blooming morsel of flesh at the apex of her sex-lips. It was like turning on a light, a surge of power ricocheted through her, so strongly she felt it in her toes, making her draw in her breath.

'Oh Nick!' she gasped as sensation took over.

The fact that he was watching excited her beyond mere arousal. Spurred on she rubbed her fingers back and forth across her clitoris, coaxing it further out, stimulating it to the point where she knew she would soon tip over the edge.

She could feel the sun through the thin cotton of

her dress, seeping into her back and adding to the body heat which was spreading through her. As she reached the peak, she tapped the hard little nub of her clitoris several times with her fingertip until her climax burst from her. Deeper and deeper the jagged fingers of sensation travelled through her, making her cry out with pleasure.

It was then that she began to move, up and down, her hips bucking, drawing Nick into the vortex with her. As the first spurt of his orgasm burst from him, Julia collapsed over him and his arms came about her. Rolling on the rug, he flipped her over on to her back and pumped his hips rapidly, driving into her as she clenched her sex muscles round him, milking him dry.

He lay, rapidly deflating inside her, his breathing ragged. Julia ran her palms soothingly over his damp back, murmuring incoherent, loving phrases in his ear as they slowly came back down to earth together.

They kissed as finally, he slipped out of her and drew her back into his arms. Within minutes, they had both drifted into a light, satiated doze.

After a while, Nick stirred.

'Are you hungry?'

He unpacked the sandwiches and shared them out, pouring them both a beakerful of the light, fruity spritzer Julia had brought in the cooler.

'What will you do,' he said after a few minutes, 'when the coffee shop closes?'

Julia frowned, reluctant to turn her mind to the unpleasant subject which had kept her awake for much of the night.

'I don't know, Nick. Start looking for another job, I suppose. What else can I do?'

'I could ask my uncle if there's anything he could offer you, if you like?'

'At the trattoria? Yes – thanks, Nick, that might help.'

He traced the pattern of the blanket thoughtfully with his fingertip.

'You know what that coffee shops needs, don't you? It needs a complete facelift and a change of image.'

'Oh? In what way?'

Nick glanced at her to check she was really listening before going on and Julia could sense he had thought about this before.

'The coffee shop is in a great position; right by the college and close to the centre of the town. And on a corner, too, so you've got all that natural light, if you took down those awful Venetian blinds. You've got your clientele right on your doorstep, all you've got to do is convince them that your place is the place they want to come to eat.'

'*My* place?'

'Why not, Julia? If you could raise the capital to buy the property you could really turn things around, make it a going concern.'

Julia shook her head, taken aback by the turn the conversation had taken.

'Go on,' she said cautiously.

'You could move into providing hot food. Good, nutritionally balanced meals. You could keep the costs down by having a daily choice of only two or three menus. That way, the students and other young people you attract could afford a good meal so when they go home to their digs at night, they only need to bother with a sandwich.'

'Sounds good so far.'

Nick grinned, leaning towards her slightly as he continued, encouraged by her response. Julia watched his face as he spoke, the way his eyes glowed with enthusiasm as he outlined his hypothetical plans, the way his mouth moved and how his hands with their long, expressive fingers were used to emphasise a point. With difficulty, she pulled her attention back to what he was saying.

'A restaurant should be more than a place to eat, it should be a meeting place, somewhere to see your friends and relax in the middle of the day. And in the evening—'

'The evening?'

'Yes – you'd want to maximise your opening times – in the evening you could stage various attractions that would appeal to your regulars. A live music night, for example. No end of students have their own bands and rarely get the chance to perform in front of an audience.'

'Steady on, Nick, aren't you getting a bit carried away? The coffee shop is tiny!'

He waved her objections away impatiently.

'You'd have a complete refit. Once you've got rid of the counters and the chill cabinets, I reckon you could comfortably fit sixty covers. You could use small, round tables for eating, and maybe fit in some upholstered units round the outside.'

'I'd need an entertainments licence, maybe even a drinks licence, not to mention planning approval. . .'

Nick sat back and grinned at her.

'Ah yes – well that's your problem . . . if you buy it.'

'How could I buy it? I don't have any money and I've never run a business in my life!'

Nick shrugged and began to pack up the picnic.

'It was just an idea. We'd better get going if we want to be on time.'

Julia helped him fold the blanket and they walked back to the car. She felt him glance at her several times as she walked, deep in thought, by his side. Given his involvement with Gavin's abortive scheme to get her back to college, Julia wouldn't put it past him to have deliberately fired her interest with his ideas for the coffee shop. She had to admit, he'd planted the germ of a plan with his hypothetical proposals and she chewed it over thoughtfully.

Melissa was waiting in the car park and Julia was forced to push her thoughts to the back of her mind. Her daughter's face was a study in consternation as she got out of Nick's van.

'What's *he* doing here?' she demanded, ignoring Julia's outstretched arms, 'Where's Dad?'

'He's on a field trip, darling, so he couldn't come. Nick very kindly offered to drive me.' She flashed Nick a smile to make up for Melissa's rudeness.

'Oh. Well I suppose at least one of you could come,' Melissa said sulkily. 'This way – you're late, you know, everyone else has started the tour. You've missed lunch.'

183

'You didn't mention anything about lunch being provided, Mel,' Julia protested, drawing level with her daughter. 'If I'd known, we'd have come straight here. We stopped for a picnic on the way, at that place we found when we brought you up here for your interview – remember?'

Julia realised at once that it was the wrong thing to say for Melissa darted a venomous look at Nick before snapping, 'I see. This is the quad.'

They toured the buildings at breakneck speed for the best part of half an hour. Melissa was brittle and frequently rude and Julia gradually became more and more dismayed. At last she caught the girl by the arm and forced her to come to a halt.

'Melissa, what on earth is wrong with you? Anyone would think you didn't want me to come.'

She literally took a step back as her daughter turned on her, her eyes flashing with temper.

'I thought you'd come with Dad! I thought he'd persuade you to go home.'

Julia felt as though Melissa had slapped her in the face. She could feel Nick standing behind her and she glanced at him pleadingly. Taking the hint, he moved away, feigning an interest in the fountains in the middle of the courtyard to give them some space.

'I'm sorry, Mel, I hadn't realised . . . I know you're finding it hard to come to terms with the fact that your father and I have separated, but—'

'You haven't *separated*, Mum – you left Dad. Don't you care that he's hurt? Don't you care about your own family any more?'

'Of course I care about you all, Mel!' Julia winced as Melissa avoided her hug. 'Oh, Melissa! I'm still your mum, and Dad's still your dad, that will never change. We don't have to be living together for that.'

'You used to be happy with him, didn't you?'

There was such a plea in the last words that Julia felt her heart squeeze in her chest.

'Yes,' she said quietly, 'I was happy. When you and Gavin were small I couldn't have been more content. But I haven't been very happy for a while, Mel, and I can't stay with your dad just so that you can feel we're both at home together while you're here.'

'So you bring your toyboy to embarrass me instead!' Melissa sneered. 'How could you flaunt him like this, a woman of your age! It's disgusting, that's what it is, *disgusting*!' Spinning on her heels she walked quickly away.

'Mel!'

Julia's distressed cry brought Nick instantly to her side. Summing up the situation in one glance, he put his hands on her shoulders and gave them a squeeze.

'Leave her, Julia, she'll get over it.'

'I can't leave her, Nick – she's important to me – she's my daughter!' Julia shouted at him, ignoring the look of shock and pain which flashed across his eyes as she pulled away from him and ran after Melissa.

She caught up with her near the canteen.

'Mel – we've got to talk.'

Melissa nodded miserably and Julia saw that there were tears on her cheeks.

'Oh, darling – come here.'

This time, Melissa did not resist her and they hugged tightly.

'It's not that I don't want you to be happy, Mum,' she sniffed, 'it's just that I don't like to see you making a fool of yourself and Nick's so much younger than you.'

They went to sit on a bench and talked for a long time. By the end, Julia felt exhausted, emotionally wrung out.

'I have to go now,' she said.

'You will think about what I've said, won't you?' Melissa pleaded. 'I only want what's best for you.'

'Do you, Mel?' Julia asked sadly.

'Of course! I do love you, Mum,' Melissa said, her voice small.

Julia looked at her daughter, remembering her as a baby and how she had watched over her as she grew up, and wondered where the years had gone. She felt old, suddenly, and tired, and she wanted nothing more than to go home. Saying good-bye to Melissa, she made her way slowly back to the car park where Nick was waiting for her in the van.

He glanced questioningly at her, but didn't say anything. Julia was grateful for his silence as they drove home, aware that he was itching to ask her what had happened.

When, at last, they reached the flat, she stopped him from getting out with her.

'I'm sorry, Nick,' she said quietly, 'but I don't want you to come up.'

'All right. I can see you need some time alone –

I'll call you tomorrow.'

'No, Nick, don't call me.'

'What?'

'I'm sorry,' she said, unable to meet his eyes. 'Melissa made me realise . . . there's no future for us, Nick and . . . I'm growing too fond of you. It would be better to stop this now, before either of us gets in too deep.'

The silence crackled between them for a moment. Then Nick spoke, his voice low and firm, sending shivers up and down her spine even in the midst of her misery.

'I can't believe you would let Melissa split us up, Julia. I love you – surely you know that by now?'

Julia squashed the leap her heart gave as he spoke and shook her head.

'It's not just Melissa. Don't you see, Nick – we might be happy for a while, but one day you're going to meet someone younger, someone you could marry and have a family with and you'll leave me. It might not be for years yet, but whenever it happens, I'm going to end up alone.'

Nick covered her cold hand where it rested on her lap and the warmth of his skin was comforting.

'I can't say how I'll feel ten years from now, Julia. But then no relationship comes with guarantees. Right now, we have a good thing going. I want us to be together, and I honestly believe that's what you want too.'

Even now, Julia could feel the familiar stirrings in the pit of her belly begin as Nick absently stroked his thumb back and forth over the back of her hand. She only had to say the word and she knew he would come upstairs with her and make love to her for so long and so exquisitely that she would forget everything but the moment.

Was that disgusting, as Melissa had said? Julia didn't think so, but she could not shake off the feeling that her daughter's words had invoked. Suddenly her beautiful affair felt grubby, sordid. She didn't know what she wanted any more.

'I'm sorry, Nick,' she whispered, close to tears.

'Don't do this, Julia,' he whispered urgently.

'I'm sorry.' Pulling her hand from beneath his, she fumbled for the door handle and made a dash for the house before he saw that she was crying.

Chapter Eleven

OVER THE NEXT few weeks, Julia deliberately kept herself busy. When Michael dragged his feet over appointing an estate agent, she took care of it. She was pleasantly surprised by the valuation, since it meant that once what was left of the mortgage was paid off, her share would be considerably more than the ten thousand pounds Michael had predicted.

She told Michael when he called round to see her and the guilty look on his face told her that he had known all along.

'Why did you lie to me?' she asked him, wondering why she didn't feel more angry than she did.

Perhaps it was that she simply didn't have the energy required for anger, she mused as he stared sullenly at her, or perhaps she just didn't care. Whatever, she cursed herself for not keeping her own finger on the pulse of their finances all these years.

'I suppose I thought you might be more

inclined to come home if you thought you wouldn't have much money behind you,' he said at last.

Julia looked at him in despair.

'That just goes to show how little you know me, Michael,' she said sadly.

Avoiding her eye, he said, 'There's no chance, then, of you changing your mind?'

Julia gazed at him and tried to summon up the slightest vestige of any feeling other than a vague, sorely tried fondness, but found she could not.

'No chance at all, Michael,' she said quietly.

He sighed and, turning towards her, he gave a small, defeated shrug.

'I'll be moving in with Gail then, after the house is sold. One of us had better live in it at least until contracts are exchanged, don't you think?'

'Undoubtedly. Can I ask you a question, Michael?'

He looked quizzically at her and Julia struggled to keep her voice neutral.

'If I'd said that, yes, I might come home, what would you have done?'

'That's a pretty pointless question in the light of what you've just said, isn't it?'

'Humour me, Michael, won't you?'

He shrugged, his whole demeanour illustrating his irritation with her.

'You're my wife. Naturally, I'd have you back.'

Julia took a deep, calming breath.

'I wonder if Gail realises that? We women are all interchangeable to you, aren't we? To you, a relationship is all about ownership and control and maintaining the *status quo*. What happened to you, Michael? I used to think you had passion in your soul – was I really so mistaken?'

Michael looked at her coldly.

'The mistake was mine, Julia, in thinking that we were suited in the first place.'

'Ouch!' She smiled at him, but his mouth merely tightened angrily in response.

'I hope you know what you've thrown away,' he told her as he left.

Julia stared at the closed door and sighed. She knew what she'd thrown away all right – something she had outgrown a long time ago. At least now she knew she needn't feel guilty about Michael any more. Gail would look after him and would no doubt be willing to be the kind of partner he wanted. Who knows? she thought wryly. In a few years we might even be able to be friends.

Now that she knew that she would shortly have some capital to play with, she began to think about her future in a new way. So many more possibilities were open to her once she had a measure of financial security. If she was careful, she could build up her capital to provide her with a reasonable pension when she retired. Or she could gamble it all on Nick's plans for the coffee shop.

Mr and Mrs Ferris had indicated that they would be delighted to sell to her. When she went to see her bank manager, more in hope than expectation, to her surprise she had been very sympathetic to Julia's ideas. If she returned with a properly drawn-up business plan, it seemed that there would be few problems with obtaining a loan for the alterations she would need to carry out.

Thinking about the coffee shop helped, in some ways, to keep her mind off Nick and how much she was missing him. At first he had written and telephoned regularly. To his credit, despite his obvious hurt, he had maintained his dignity all along, but his quiet stoicism had been more than Julia could bear and eventually she had begged him not to continue. She threw herself into her plans as they began to take shape in her mind, finally deciding that yes – she would go for it.

Yet while she coped mentally, she could not school her body to not miss Nick. There was a literal physical ache in her chest every time she thought about him and an insistent, needy pulse beat between her thighs as she dreamed of feeling his body close to hers again.

In the dark, lonely hours of the night, when the tight rein she held on herself was loosened by the onset of sleep, she often reached for him. Finding his place empty, her fingers would creep, half-unconsciously, to the moist, warm centre of her which yearned for his touch, his lips, his maleness. Allowing herself to drift, in that dreamy halfway state between sleep and wakefulness, she would let her fingers stroke gently along the eager folds of her sex, comforting, exciting, making her body ready for the loving she knew it would not receive.

Slowly, slowly, the feelings would build while Julia focused her mind on the memory of Nick's face, the scent of his skin, unique to him, on the feel of his fingers as he caressed her. And she would come, inevitably with a small sob for as soon as the waves of ecstasy ebbed away, she was left feeling more alone, more empty than she had felt before.

Much as she tried to hide it, everyone around her noticed her distraction, from the girls at the coffee shop to Gavin.

'What's the point, Mum?' he asked her soon after it had happened. 'You're miserable, Nick's miserable – why don't you just relax about everything? Melissa will come round in her own time.'

But Julia just shook her head and closed her mind to his arguments.

'It isn't just what Melissa said,' she tried to explain. 'It simply wouldn't work, not the way I'd want it to.'

She hadn't allowed Gavin to pursue the subject, but did not stop him from talking about Nick when he visited. Apparently he had taken the extra exams he had stayed on at college an additional term to sit and was now looking for a job whilst helping out in his uncle's trattoria when the need arose.

Julia was secretly grateful to Gavin for subtly letting her know that Nick was all right. That way she didn't have to admit to anyone, least of all herself, just how much she missed him.

One Sunday lunchtime shortly before Christmas she meandered down the stairs with the vague idea that she would take a short walk in the winter sunshine. Contracts were due to be exchanged on the lease to the coffee shop early the following week and she had already heard that her loan had been approved. Both Carolyn and Sally had accepted her offer of part-time work, once she opened and she had spent hours devising menus and working out ideas to draw the customers in.

She was aware that she should have been feeling excited, standing as she was on the threshold of an entire new venture, but somehow without someone to share her feelings with, she felt, if she was honest, a bit flat. So when Fenella waylaid her on her way out, she was heartily glad of the diversion.

'Have you got a minute, Julia?'

'Yes, of course.'

Julia followed her landlady into the sitting-room, her curiosity pricked. Fenella was in her painting overalls and it wasn't often she was seen outside the studio in those. She seemed ill at ease, pouring two glasses of dry sherry and handing Julie one without thinking to ask if she'd like it.

'I wondered if you might do me a small favour, if you're free today?'

Julia, pleased at the prospect of having something positive to do, jumped at the chance.

'Certainly. It must be awkward for you sometimes now that Greg's spending so much time at Kerry's house. You mustn't hesitate to ask me if I can help, you know.'

'Er, well, that's very nice of you, Julia, but actually what I had in mind for this afternoon isn't something that I would normally ask Greg to help me with.'

'Oh?'

194

Julia was intrigued. The normally unflappable Fenella looked positively shifty as she knocked back her sherry and gazed out of the window, as if hoping to find inspiration in the garden.

'The fact is, I was commissioned some time ago to produce a series of sketches and paintings for a private collector. I've almost finished, but for the last few sketches, I need a second model.'

Julia laughed.

'You want *me* to model for you? Really, Fenella, I'm flattered, but—'

'You'd be masked,' Fenella cut in hastily, 'so your anonymity would be completely preserved. I wouldn't ask you, but my regular female model has phoned to say she's caught this wretched flu bug. I'd wait until next week, but Darren is away then and two weeks' delay would really mean I'd stand no chance of meeting my deadline.'

Gradually, Julia was putting two and two together. The mention of a mask and Darren, the young, nude male whose portrait Fenella had shown her made her jaw drop.

'Why Fenella,' she said at last, 'are you trying to tell me you're producing erotic drawings? You are!' She laughed delightedly as Fenella went pink.

'They are very tasteful – and very expensive!' she said defensively.

'I'm sure they are! Okay, Fenella – it sounds like fun! I certainly haven't got anything better to do this sunny Sunday afternoon. Lead on and show me what you want me to wear!'

Whatever she had been expecting, it wasn't quite this . . . kinky, Julia reflected as she stood, stripped to her undies, behind a screen in Fenella's studio. She should have twigged when she walked in and saw Darren reclining on the couch flicking through a copy of a computer magazine, naked apart from a pair of indecently thin, red silk boxer shorts.

Fenella, fortified by the sherry and over her initial embarrassment, bustled about the studio, setting up her easel and pencils and checking the light. Julia eyed the black, shiny leather corset and the pouch which passed for a pair of briefs and grimaced. Very little was going to be left to the imagination once she was encased in these.

'Come on, girl,' she said to herself, 'don't be such a wimp!'

'Do you need any help behind there?' Fenella called out cheerfully and Darren looked up hopefully.

'No, I can manage!' Julia replied hastily, stripping off her underwear and folding the corset around her body.

The black leather was silk-lined. It felt soft against her bare skin as she began to fasten the hooks and eyes which, thankfully, ran up the front. The garment was so tight it pushed her breasts up and together, so that when she looked down she saw a deep, inviting cleavage which she had never seen before. Was that really her body, so enticingly displayed? Julia felt the warmth creep upward from her toes, her mind raced with the possibilites which could arise from wearing such an outfit.

Her waist was enclosed as if in an iron fist, but once she became used to the constriction, Julia did not find the sensation unpleasant. In fact, she rather liked the way the boning moulded her womanly curves into a perfect hourglass. Her hips flared dramatically from her waist and the rounded globes of her buttocks were thrown into sharp relief.

The shiny black panties barely covered her mound and the deep cleft between her buttocks, but once she had adjusted them to her satisfaction, Julia found they were surprisingly comfortable. There was an unopened pack of stockings on the chair and she rolled them up her legs carefully, fearful of snagging the delicate, cobweb-fine fabric.

'Oh yes – that looks gorgeous!'

Julia almost jumped out of her skin as Fenella's face appeared at the top of the screen and she flushed guiltily, knowing the other woman had seen her admiring the way her legs looked in the luxurious stockings.

'Um . . . what do I wear on my feet?' she stammered, feeling awkward.

'See if those boots fit, then come out and I'll give you the mask.'

The boots which, Julia now saw, were leaning against the chair, were shiny red plastic, thigh-length with impossibly high, spiky heels and viciously pointed toes. She was glad to find they were a size too large, for it meant that her toes avoided being cramped by the tapering ends.

There was a full-length mirror bolted to the wall and Julia regarded herself critically in it. She looked good, shockingly so and she was taken by surprise by the swift dart of desire which ran through her belly. She had never thought of herself as particularly narcissistic, but then she had never had the opportunity before to dress up in such an outlandish outfit.

She emerged from behind the screen almost shyly, conscious of Darren's eyes on her as she presented herself to Fenella. Darren gave a long, low whistle between his teeth and Fenella snapped, 'That's enough of that – this is art, not a peep show!'

Julia stifled the urge to giggle at Fenella's ferocious stance and took the feathered mask which was offered to her. It was a half face mask, covering her eyes and the upper part of her nose, but leaving the lower half of her face bare. Attaching it to her hair, she stroked her fingers across the soft, dark feathers, admiring the beautiful colouring, black and smoke-grey with an occasional flash of deep, dark red.

'Here—' Fenella smiled at her, '– a good slick of red lipstick for the finishing touch.'

After she had applied it, Julia stared at her expression with something akin to awe. She barely recognised herself in the straight-backed, strutting dominatrix in the feathered mask who stared back at her from the mirror.

'Right, Julia,' Fenella said briskly, 'if you wouldn't mind standing here, over Darren. . .'

Julia stood as she was asked, legs astride the supine form of the beautiful young man whom Fenella had arranged on the floor. Fists on hips, Julia towered over him in her high heels, tilting her head to just the angle Fenella wanted before the other woman settled behind her easel.

'That's it! I knew you'd be good at this Julia, but I hadn't realised you'd be a natural! No, don't laugh – it'll only take a few minutes to sketch you and I don't want you to move.'

Because there was nowhere else for her to look, Julia studied the young man lying beneath her. He gazed up at her with calculating blue eyes, his expression leaving her in no doubt that he found her get-up powerfully arousing. Julia felt a flutter in the soft flesh between her thighs and she narrowed her eyes.

The red silk boxer shorts were stretched tight over Darren's crotch, clinging almost lovingly to the outline of his semi-hard penis. He seemed totally unembarrassed by the state of his arousal, in fact Julia could swear that his pupils dilated as he saw that she was looking at him.

Their eyes met and Julia felt the awareness which passed between them like little stabs of electricity running up and down her body. This beautiful young man desired her – he was hers for the taking.

'Right – let's take advantage of that nice erection, Darren,' Fenella said matter-of-factly, breaking into Julia's thoughts. 'Could you just rest the spike of your heel against Darren's penis, Julia? I know it's uncomfortable, but I only want to make a quick sketch of the boot and the boxers. Perhaps that's what I should call it, eh? "Boot and Boxers".'

Julia posed as she was asked, noticing the way Darren's cock hardened the instant the dangerous tip of her heel pressed gently against the engorged flesh, protected only by the flimsy silk of his boxers. Listening to Fenella's cheerful, down-to-earth banter whilst witnessing Darren's increasing arousal, Julia felt as if she had stepped into some bizarre, surreal stage set.

Just as the muscles in her calves began to protest at being kept poised for so long, Fenella said she could relax. For the best part of an hour, Julia followed Fenella's instructions to the letter. She posed, whip in hand, Darren on his knees before her. Her eyes focused on the gleam of the handcuffs which encircled his wrists behind his back and she wondered how the afternoon would end.

Darren had made it perfectly clear, by his body language and the hot, hopeful expression in his eyes, that he would gladly re-enact these scenes with her for real, given half the chance. Julia could not deny that she was turned on too. There was something deliciously wicked in camping it up like this. She imagined the young man now pressing his lips against the pointed toe of her boot unhooking the corset which held her body so erect and burying his face in the cleft between her breasts. In her mind's eye she saw herself exploring his firm young body with fingers, lips and tongue, tasting the sweat she could see gleaming on the surface of his skin, sampling the firm, juicy taste of him as she peeled down the boxer shorts. . .

'Julia? Julia, you can get changed now.'

It took a moment or two for Fenella's voice to penetrate the erotic fug in her mind. Julia shook her head to clear it and stepped back, away from Darren. He was sitting on the couch now, his body tense, expectant, waiting for her to decide what she wanted to do.

She had only to say the word and he would follow her upstairs. She could enjoy his body for an hour or two and send him away when she felt refreshed. After all, wasn't that what she had set out to do when she left Michael? Rejuvenate herself?

Slowly, she took off the mask and handed it to Fenella.

'Thanks, Julia,' the older woman said warmly. 'I owe you one. You were great, wasn't she, Darren?'

Julia's eyes met Darren's and he stared meaningfully at her.

'Yeah,' he agreed, his voice deep and throaty. 'Really great.'

And suddenly she knew. Pleasant though it might be, making love to the willing, virile young man before her, she didn't want the plain mechanics of sex. If she took Darren upstairs with her she would go through the motions, probably have a highly satisfactory orgasm, the effects of which would last a full half-hour before she became restless again.

It wouldn't be enough. It could never be enough. Sex, by itself, was not what she wanted. She wanted sex with someone she cared about. With Nick.

'Thank you,' she said, calmly acknowledging the implied compliment. 'It was a pleasure to work with you, Darren.'

Smiling coolly at him, she saw that he recognised her rejection and regretted it, yet there was no rancour in his expression. Slipping back behind the screen, Julia undressed quickly, emerging in her own clothes feeling much calmer than she had in quite a while.

'Would you like to stay down for dinner, Julia? It's the least I could do after you've stepped in like this.'

Shaking her head, Julia smiled at Fenella.

'That's very kind of you, Fenella, but I have to go and see someone.'

Fenella glanced at her shrewdly and nodded.

'Good for you,' she said softly.

Impulsively, Julia stepped forward and kissed her on the cheek.

'Thanks, Fenella,' she said softly.

'For what?'

Julia shrugged.

'I don't know. Making me feel good about myself again?'

Fenella laughed.

'Go on with you. Be happy.'

'I intend to be!' Julia retorted, slipping through the door and closing it behind her with a quiet, decisive 'click'.

Chapter Twelve

SOME OF JULIA'S new-found optimism left her as she stepped off the bus at the end of Nick's street. Supposing he didn't want to see her after all these weeks? Suppose he had someone else?

Her steps faltered and she seriously contemplated turning back. He might not even be in, for goodness' sake – he could be visiting his parents, or working at the trattoria. . .

Pull yourself together! she lectured herself ruthlessly. You came here to tell Nick that you realise now that you made a mistake and you're damn well going to go through with it. If he's embarrassed by you, or doesn't want to know, at least you'll have the satisfaction of knowing that you tried to put things right.

As she walked along the street, Julia found herself hurrying, oblivious to the rain which had begun to fall, eager to see him now that she had made the decision to come. She wanted to tell him all about the coffee shop, and to share with him all her hopes and anxieties about the venture.

But, most of all, she simply wanted to feel him in her arms again, to run her fingers through the soft fall of his hair and to hear him whisper her name.

Still feeling the effects of her earlier arousal, Julia let her mind run riot through the whole gamut of erotic possibilities in their meeting. By the time she arrived at the house she was on a slow burn, just waiting for Nick to light the fuse which would make her catch light.

She was slightly breathless after running up the stairs to his flat. Raindrops dripped from the ends of her hair, steaming gently as they encountered the heat of her skin. Gathering all her courage, she knocked on his door, praying that he would be in and that he would be alone.

He was. His eyes widened momentarily as he opened the door and saw her standing there. With one glance, Julia took in the tired circles under his eyes and the slight downward turn to his lips which she'd never noticed before.

'Nick. . .?'

He seemed to recover himself, stepping aside to let her in. There was a book lying open beside the sofa and soft music playing on the CD player. Julia pictured him as he had been seconds earlier, stretched out on the sofa, relaxed, alone and she felt consumed with lust.

Turning to him, she unbuttoned her raincoat and let it fall to the floor. He watched her, a wariness in his eyes which she longed to dispel. Without saying a word, she pulled her top up over her head and threw it aside. She heard his sharp intake of breath as she saw that she was naked underneath and drew down the zip of her jeans. Hooking her thumbs in the waistband, she pulled them down and kicked them aside with her socks, so that she was facing him in nothing but her plain, white cotton panties.

Still he did not speak, or make a move towards her and Julia's nerves stretched to screaming pitch. Refusing to listen to the small, malevolent voice in her head which said perhaps he didn't want her any more, she stepped tentatively towards him.

She could feel the tension in him before she touched him, could sense the barely leashed passion running hotly through his blood. Biting her lower lip, she slowly put out her hand and touched him lightly on the top of one shoulder.

She had half expected that he would flinch away from her. When he did not, she felt emboldened. Stepping slightly closer to him, she absorbed the familiar heat of his body across the few inches which separated them. Julia ran her palm down to cover his left breast, holding it against his heart and revelling in its acceleration.

'Julia—'

'Ssh!'

She put her hand gently over his mouth, caging his words. She was afraid to hear them, scared that he might make her stop, even send her away.

The cool air in the room had made her nipples harden and bloom so that their sensitive tips brushed lightly against the soft cotton of his T-shirt. Julia could feel her flesh quiver, and the secret well of her desire seeped fresh moisture. The smell of arousal, hers and his, filled the air, a potent spur to the senses.

Nick was watching her, his eyes dark, his emotions hidden. He could not hide the reaction her nearness had provoked though and Julia was aware of a deep, satisfying pleasure as she closed her hand over the hard, denim-encased rod which strained against the front of his jeans.

There was something powerfully erotic about standing, virtually naked, so close to a fully dressed man. She felt . . . vulnerable, certainly, and trusting in a way she had never felt before. She was aware that she was laying herself open to him, inviting his rejection.

Opening her mouth, she leaned forward and pressed her lips against the skin of his throat. It was damp and slippery and she darted out her tongue to taste the saltiness which lay on the surface. Standing on tiptoe, she kissed the corners of his mouth, making him sigh. His sweet breath tickled over her skin, his eyes following her every move as she drew back to look at him.

His arms hung loosely by his sides. Julia picked up one of his hands and held it between both of hers. She loved his hands – they were strong and smooth with long, square-tipped fingers which could be so sensitive. Bringing his hand up to her face, she nuzzled his palm with her cheek, holding his gaze as she drew the tip of his forefinger between her lips.

Nick was unable to control his sharp intake of breath as she began to suck on it, drawing it slowly into the warm, wet cavern of her mouth, up to the first knuckle. Her tongue swirled around its end, flicking at its underside before she took more of it inside her mouth, her eyes half

206

closing as she imagined it was his beautiful cock nudging the inside of her cheeks.

Nick was clearly sharing her imaginings for he groaned softly, closing his eyes briefly against her. When he opened them again she was thrilled by the iridescent glow in their depths as he looked at her.

Gently removing his finger from her mouth, Nick brought both hands up to cup her face, pressing her cheeks so that her mouth opened automatically to admit his marauding tongue. He plundered her mouth with an urgency which sparked an answering desperation in her.

His touch was not gentle as it passed over her body, shaping her back, squeezing her breasts together then letting them spring apart as his hands roamed to her waist and the gentle thrust of her buttocks. Impatiently, he dispensed with her panties, burying his face briefly, shockingly, in the damp curls between her thighs and breathing in the scent of her as if reminding himself of it.

His mouth was no less demanding than his hands as he licked and kissed and nibbled his way up her body, his tongue swirling round her navel and up, up until he reached her breasts. Julia moaned softly as he lathed each hard crest with his tongue, coaxing them into ever hardening peaks.

He did not object as Julia pulled his T-shirt out of the waistband of his jeans and pushed it up, impatient to feel the silken heat of his bare skin against her breasts. He pulled it off and crushed her to him, his mouth finding hers again as he unfastened his jeans and pushed them down.

They were both hot, their skin slick with sweat.

Breathing hard, they sank down on to the hard floor, kissing and biting, rolling together in a tangle of arms and legs, as if wrestling rather than making love.

He entered her, just like that, without so much as a passing attention to her sensitive vulval flesh. It didn't matter; Julia was ready for him, her passage slick and welcoming, drawing him in and holding him close to her. Her nails scored the vulnerable skin of his back as he drove into her, holding her buttocks in his hands and pressing her pelvis tightly against his.

'Julia – oh Christ – Julia!'

He threw back his head as he came, his face contorted with an ecstasy which looked very close to pain as he thrust into her. It seemed to go on and on, burst after burst of hot fluid which filled and fulfilled her. Wrapping her ankles round his waist, Julia hung on to him as long as possible, dreading the moment when he would, inevitably, pull away.

When, at last, he did, he looked down at her, his expression troubled.

'So – what was all that about?'

Julia frowned, feeling horribly exposed suddenly as the warmth of his body was removed from her.

'What do you mean?'

Nick shrugged with a nonchalance Julia was convinced he was far from feeling.

'After all this time – why the sudden lust for my body?'

It was an understandable reaction, she supposed, but it still hurt. Taking a deep breath, she said calmly, 'I came to tell you that I'm sorry. I should never have sent you away.'

Nick regarded her warily, as if he wanted to believe her but could not quite bring himself to do so.

'No, you shouldn't,' he agreed, an edge of petulance creeping into his voice.

Julia smiled tentatively.

'Please – Nick – help me. I don't know how to show you . . . won't you love me a little? Please?'

They gazed at each other for a long moment and Julia was relieved to see a softening in his eyes.

'And if I don't want to?' he said, his voice mildly teasing.

'Then I'll simply have to lie here on your living-room floor and satisfy myself.' She groaned at the gleam in his eye, knowing she was hoist with her own petard. 'No, Nick, don't be cruel! I've had no one but myself to pleasure me for weeks now.'

'Really?' he said, serious now.

Julia stared at him and realised it was important to him that she had stayed faithful during the long weeks of their separation.

'Really,' she confirmed softly.

He smiled then and she was glad that she had resisted temptation earlier that morning. No one could love her like Nick did and she had a feeling that he would not need much more persuading. She was right.

Leaping to his feet, he reached down and scooped her up into his arms. Laughing, she lay her head against his chest as he carried her through to the bedroom and laid her carefully on top of the rumpled sheets. He stared down at her for several seconds.

'What is it?' she whispered, feeling vulnerable again.

He shook his head, making the golden waves of his hair ripple on his shoulders.

'I can't believe you're here.'

Julia grinned, relieved.

'Believe it!' she told him.

'I want to touch you, to kiss every square centimetre of your body to convince myself you're not an apparition.'

'Be my guest!'

He leaned over her on the bed, supporting himself on his hands which he placed either side of her head, on the pillows.

'Be sure you mean that,' he said, his voice low and mock-threatening.

Julia shivered, anticipating his next move.

'I do,' she replied, unable to speak in more than a whisper.

She closed her eyes as he began to kiss her – first her temples and her cheeks, then her closed eyelids and the tip of her nose. His tongue licked delicately along the join between her lips on his way to her earlobes, then the sensitive flesh behind her ears.

His kisses there sent delicious shudders running right down to her toes, bringing her skin up in goosebumps. Nick chuckled throatily, working his way down her neck to the point where her collar bones joined. Little butterfly kisses just above the bone made her shiver with delight.

Her breasts quivered in anticipation as he dipped his head and trailed a path across her chest, but he left them alone, choosing instead to nip and kiss his way to the junction between her body and her shoulder. Julia gasped as his tongue delved into the moist crevice of her armpit before his lips moved down her arm, seeking out the tender crease of her elbow.

It amazed her that such gentle eroticism should bring her so close to climax, yet she had to admit that she was closer to that state now than she had ever been with any other man even at the point of penetration.

She sighed as he kissed the gentle underswell of each breast, aware that her nipples were thrusting upward, yearning for his kiss. It did not come, instead he nuzzled the soft mound of her stomach before swooping down the bed to her knees. He worked his way downwards, kissing and sucking gently at her skin until he reached her ankles.

His tongue teased the sensitive spot beside her heel bone before brushing his lips across the top of her foot to her toes. Slowly, as if savouring a gourmet feast, he sucked each of her toes in turn. Julia had never realised before that there was an invisible thread connecting her toes to her womb, but she felt its pull now.

Gradually, almost of their own volition, her thighs fell open to reveal the moist, pouting lips of her sex. Nick opened her with his thumbs, exposing her highly sensitive innermost flesh to his gaze before dipping his head to kiss her there.

Julia gasped, hardly able to bear it as his lips

nibbled and caressed her, his tongue jabbing delicately at the entrance to her body.

'Oh, oh yes!' she breathed as he swirled his stiffened tongue around her entrance. 'Put it inside me, Nick. . .'

He obliged and she contracted her muscles round him, trying to hold on to his roving tongue, but he would not let her. Greedily, he lapped at their combined juices, opening her wider with his thumbs and rubbing his nose against her burgeoning clitoris. Drawing the juices out of her body, he used them to lubricate her reddening sex-lips still more until her entire vulva was wet and slippery and ready for him.

Now he concentrated all his attention on the tiny nub of flesh whose capacity for pleasure was far out of proportion to its size. Shamelessly, Julia raised her hips off the bed, pressing herself against his lips and he nibbled at her most sensitive flesh.

'Please, Nick, please. . .!'

Almost incoherent with desire, she opened her legs wider and pushed out her clit, bearing down on to his rapidly moving tongue until at last her climax broke. Hearing her sharp intake of breath, Nick gripped her bottom with both hands and pressed his face against her sex. Just as she reached the very peak of her orgasm, he bit gently on the quivering stem of flesh.

Julia went wild, thrashing her head from side to side and grinding her sex against his teeth. On and on it went, the most intense sensations rolling in waves throughout her entire body until she collapsed, exhausted, against the pillows.

'Julia? Julia – darling – are you all right?'

He kissed her eyes, her hair, her chin, his hands gentle against her skin as he stroked and calmed her. It took a huge effort on Julia's part to nod and reassure him, and several more minutes before she could summon the strength to open her eyes and smile at him.

'Julia . . . don't cry . . . please don't cry. . .'

Until he spoke, Julia hadn't realised that there were tears on her cheeks. Nick sounded close to tears himself. Shaking her head helplessly, she reached up and held him to her, burying her face in his hair and breathing in its clean fragrance.

She didn't need words to communicate to him what she wanted now, she merely manoeuvred her hips so that she was underneath him before opening her thighs and guiding him in to her warm, wet haven.

This time there was no thrust of possession, no taking one of the other. Rather they came together in a gentle loving which soothed and calmed them after the storms of the previous hour. Nick did not pump in and out of her, they remained locked, thighs entwined, pelvises rocking in unison.

This gentle motion set up a deep, ever increasing vibration which grew and consumed them, finally tipping them both over the edge into a mutually satisfying release.

When, at last, they finally peeled apart, Julia felt suffused with a warm glow. She could see her own intense satisfaction mirrored in the depths of Nick's calm grey eyes and she felt happy in a way that she could not ever remember feeling before.

They lay, content and sated, in each other's

arms for a long time. Nick stroked Julia's hair intermittently. Every now and again, Julia pressed her lips against his chest where she could feel his heart beating strongly beneath his skin.

After a while, Nick broke the silence.

'Does this mean we go on as before?'

Julia raised herself up slightly so that she could see his face.

'Do you want to?'

Nick gazed at her steadily.

'I never wanted anything else.'

Julia smiled.

'Nor did I, not really.'

She traced the light whorls of hair on his chest with her forefinger.

'I took your advice,' she said after a while.

'Oh?' he said lazily.

'Yes. You know – about the coffee shop? I bought the lease.'

Nick looked at her in surprise.

'Really?'

'Yes. I got a loan from the bank to help pay for the alterations. I was wondering if you'd be interested in helping me?'

Nick shrugged slightly, though Julia could tell he was flattered that she had asked him.

'I've precious little else to do.'

'Thanks.'

She settled back on to his chest with a small, contented sigh. Nick's body began to soften and relax as he drifted off to sleep. Just as he began to doze, Julia spoke again.

'Nick?'

'Hmm?'

'Nick . . . I was wondering . . . the coffee shop isn't going to be very grand or anything, but it's a start. Do you think . . . would you like to come and cook for me?'

He pulled back from the verge of sleep and looked at her.

'Is that what you want?'

'Only if you do too – but yes, that's what I want.'

He smiled at her then, that open, slightly lop sided grin which had endeared him to her from the first moment she saw him.

'Then I would be honoured to come and work for you.'

'Not *for* me, Nick, *with* me. We'd be partners – you'd cook, I'd run things.'

'Okay. What about us?'

Julia reached up and kissed him lightly on the lips.

'I thought we'd take each day as it comes. Enjoy what we have for as long as it lasts. Does that sound sensible to you?'

'Infinitely. One day at a time – who knows what the future holds?'

He kissed her, the glint in his eye telling her that he was as keen as she was to make their future a joint venture.

'So, this coffee shop of ours – what's it to be called? *Julia's*?'

Julia shook her head.

'I was thinking . . . if it's all right with you . . . I thought *Lowther's* has a rather classy ring to it. What do you think?'

'I think,' said Nick, rolling on to his side and

cupping her breast with his hand, 'that we ought to seal our partnership with more than just a handshake.'

'Oh?' she said mischievously, smiling up at him. 'What exactly did you have in mind?'

He kissed her forehead, each cheek, the bridge of her nose and her chin.

'I think,' he said, between kisses, 'that I shall enjoy persuading you that we have a future together.'

He captured her mouth with his and slipped his fingers into the somnolent flesh between her legs. Already she was moist and warm, responding to his touch with an eagerness which never failed to excite him.

'Mmm,' he sighed, his breath hot in her ear, 'I think I know just the way to persuade you that *Lowther's* needs two Lowthers to be worthy of the name!'

'But Nick—'

'Ssh!' His tongue swirled around one hardening nipple while his fingers slipped easily inside her. 'Open your legs to me, my darling,' he whispered, 'and resign yourself to my persuasion!'

With a low sigh of surrender Julia parted her thighs and did just that.

[ ]	Back in Charge	Mariah Greene	£4.99
[ ]	The Discipline of Pearls	Susan Swann	£4.99
[ ]	The Ritual of Pearls	Susan Swann	£4.99
[ ]	Hotel Aphrodisia	Dorothy Starr	£4.99
[ ]	Arousing Anna	Nina Sheridan	£4.99
[ ]	Playing the Game	Selina Seymour	£4.99
[ ]	The Women's Club	Vanessa Davies	£4.99
[ ]	A Slave to His Kiss	Anastasia Dubois	£4.99
[ ]	Saturnalia	Zara Devereux	£4.99
[ ]	Shopping Around	Mariah Greene	£4.99
[ ]	Inspiration	Stephanie Ash	£4.99
[ ]	Dark Secret	Marina Anderson	£4.99

X Libris offers an eXciting range of quality titles which can be ordered from the following address:

Little, Brown and Company (UK),
P.O. Box 11,
Falmouth,
Cornwall TR10 9EN

Alternatively you may fax your order to the above address.
FAX No. 01326 317444.

Payments can be made as follows: cheque, postal order (payable to Little, Brown and Company) or by credit cards, Visa/Access. Do not send cash or currency. UK customers and B.F.P.O. please allow £1.00 for postage and packing for the first book, plus 50p for the second book, plus 30p for each additional book up to a maximum charge of £3.00 (7 books plus).

Overseas customers including Ireland please allow £2.00 for the first book plus £1.00 for the second book, plus 50p for each additional book.

NAME (Block Letters) _____

_____

ADDRESS _____

_____

_____

☐ I enclose my remittance for _____

☐ I wish to pay by Access/Visa card

Number _____

Card Expiry Date _____